Sterling Place

Sterling Place

Ray Garcia

To order additional copies of this book, contact:
Xlibris
844-714-8691
www.Xlibris.com
Orders@Xlibris.com
565215

For Immediate Release
Tuesday, December 20, 1960
The Civil Aeronautics Board
Washington, DC

CAB member Mr. G. Joseph Minetti, who will head up the Board of Inquiry into the December 16 midair collision over New York City at public hearings beginning January 4, 1961, in Brooklyn, today issued the following statement:

> "The Civil Aeronautics Board is now engaged in one of the most comprehensive accident investigations in its history. After this investigation is completed, and the evidence developed at the public hearing has been evaluated, the Board will issue its findings, setting forth the probable cause of this accident."

Introduction

The investigation into the cause of the collision between Trans-World Airline Flight 266 and United Airlines Flight 826 would draw a battlefront of accusations and counter accusations of incompetence between representatives of United Airlines and the Federal Aviation Administration. In the end, it would bring about changes to both parties, changes that remain today. Nevertheless, even though over forty-nine years have passed since the accident occurred, the debate continues: What factor or factors caused United Airlines Flight 826 to continue beyond the Preston intersection? Who was at fault? Was there a cover-up, and, if so, by whom and why?

Synopsis

During a dinner with friends in Connecticut, the topic of John Kennedy Jr.'s death came up. News of his death in a plane crash had stunned the world, and since I had pilot training, I was immediately asked many questions. One particularly interesting one was why do planes collide when there is so much air space?

As I tried to answer the question, I couldn't help but think of that horrifying December day when two planes did just that. It was the holiday season, one of the busiest times for commercial flying. With just nine days left before Christmas, Americans were taking to the skies to be with their loved ones. I always believed Christmas was a holy occasion. It's a time of giving, a time to thank the Lord, and a time to love one another. Nothing should go wrong, but it did.

On Friday, December 16, 1960, a Trans-World Airline plane, the Lockheed Constellation, and a United DC-8 jetliner collided in a blinding snowfall over Staten Island, New York, killing all 128 occupants aboard both planes, as well as six on the ground, making this the worst air disaster in aviation history. TWA Flight 266 had departed Columbus Airport with a crew of five and thirty-nine passengers, including two infants. Their destination was LaGuardia Airport in New York. United Flight 826 had originated as Flight 856 in Los Angeles, with a crew of three: Captain Robert H. Sawyer, First Officer Robert W. Fiebing, and Second Officer Richard E. Prewitt. They departed Los Angeles at approximately 3:20 a.m., inbound for Chicago, where they would pick up the rest of the crew and passengers for their final destination, Idlewild International Airport, New York, now known as JFK.

When the planes were fifteen minutes from their destinations, both were ordered by air traffic controllers to hold their positions over New Jersey. TWA 266 held a pattern of five thousand feet over Linden, and United 826 held position six thousand feet over the Preston. Officials later stated that the TWA plane had been cleared to leave its holding pattern and make its landing approach when its last message was heard. Its flight path called for it to go across New Jersey, pass a checkpoint off Coney Island, and then fly over the Prospect Park section of Brooklyn toward LaGuardia. When United DC-8 got permission to make its landing approach, it was to pass a checkpoint off the Rockaway's and fly over Rockaway Beach and Jamaica Bay to Idlewild.

The ceiling for that day was six hundred feet; visibility was a mile. Visibility beyond that was minimal. According to reports issued by the Federal Aviation Administration and the Civil Aeronautic Board, both planes were under instrument flight rules, yet something went terribly wrong. With Captain Robert H. Sawyer at the controls, the DC-8 passed its assigned vector; perhaps he was disoriented, as he was flying with only one VOR (a very high-frequency omni-directional range). The instrument flight data recorder indicates that the crew had changed airspeed seven times within minutes and that the plane reached speeds of over four hundred miles per hour and was eleven miles off course. LaGuardia radar indicated that the two planes made contact at approximately 10:33 a.m., over Miller Army Airfield in Staten Island, New York. After the collision, one plane continued northeast for a distance of eight or ten miles. The other appeared to be nearly stationary for a moment, then commenced a slow right turn to a southwesterly heading and disappeared from radar. The Constellation fell in three parts over Staten Island, bodies spewing from its fuselage as it tumbled toward the ground, indicating that the propeller-driven plane had been rammed broadside. The crew of the DC-8 fought to land the crippled jet at Prospect Park, but the badly damaged plane fell onto a populated area of Brooklyn, disintegrating on impact and obliterating everything in its path.

It was a very cold morning, and there was a gusting wind, making it difficult to walk. The falling snow had turned to freezing rain, making it difficult to see. Snowbanks from the previous day lined the streets. My parents didn't know I was on my way to Flatbush Avenue in Brooklyn to look at some bikes. I was only fifteen and not allowed to travel in the trains by myself, so this would be a new experience. I was window-shopping when a thunderous explosion shook the ground. There was a moment of silence that seemed to last an eternity. Suddenly, people were running toward Seventh

Avenue. Someone yelled that a building had collapsed. I ran with them to see. When I reached Seventh Avenue, I stopped and stared, too young to understand the magnitude of what surrounded me. A chilling sensation gripped my entire body, for this wasn't just a building that came down. This was worse, much worse. This is my story . . .

Route 9 South, New Jersey
February 10, 2001
10:45 a.m.

When I think of New Jersey, I think of Route 9. I used to drive Route 9 every Saturday in my early years as a student pilot. Every Saturday, I would hop into my old car, go through the Holland Tunnel into New Jersey, get onto Route 9, and head out to the airport in Linden for my flying lessons with my instructor Vincent Koch. Vince was a quiet man of about thirty, and very smart as an instructor pilot. He had both the patience and the skills. I was always the first student to arrive. We would usually have a ten-minute session about what he wanted me to do that day. He would give me assignments to prepare me for the two hours of flight training. With Vince you had to be prepared.

I remember getting ready for my first cross-country flight one summer morning. I had prepared myself, both physically and mentally, for over two weeks and I was ready. Our trip was to Wilkes-Barre Airport in Pennsylvania. Our estimated time for the eighty-three-mile trip was forty-two minutes; we would be flying at seven thousand feet with a ground speed of 118 miles per hour. Arriving at the Linden Airport, I did what I always did: I signed in, got the keys to the plane, went to pre-flight it, and reported back to Vince. When he walked into the conference room, I already had the map plotted out and had checked the winds at that altitude for that day. He approved my preparation and we talked of what to expect at the Wilkes Barre Airport, since I had never been there before. At that time, Wilkes Barre was home to Eastern Airlines, so we knew there would be heavy air traffic. Management gave the okay; I called in the flight plan to the Flight Service Station, and headed out toward the red-and-white Cessna 150 I would be piloting. I went through my checklist, called out clear, and cranked my engine to life.

As I was taxiing out to the active runway, I could see that I had a perfect day before me. Uni-com cleared us for immediate takeoff. I looked at Vince as he mentioned, let's go. With throttle to full power, the plane roared down the four-thousand-foot runway. As I steered the plane down the broken white lines, I remembered what Vince had once said to me that, next to him, I had the best takeoffs and landings he had ever seen, although he felt my landings were better than my takeoffs. He always enjoyed my final approaches, and often said I had a good approach. On reaching takeoff speed, I gently pulled back on the yoke as we broke gravity and left Mother Earth. Twenty minutes later, we were cruising at seven thousand feet. The round trip took four hours. I felt proud that day, wishing my father had been alive for he would have been proud too. Learning how to fly gave me discipline and character, but I couldn't have done it without Vincent Koch, and his patience. Thanks, Vincent, wherever you are.

I have always been fascinated with airplanes, especially the airliners, with their mammoth size and the power they generate. For me, flying was a way of isolating myself from the outside world. I would rent a little Cessna 150 and climb to four thousand feet, follow the New Jersey Turnpike, and just laze around the open space, soaring through the sky like a bird and without any worry in the world. I could see the automobile traffic beneath me. Looking down the front of the plane's nose, I would see miles and miles of traffic. It was good to be above it all. I would observe the early-morning-sun rising over the horizon—what a view! I always respected that little airport, and the folks who took pride in it. That was 1976.

In 1957, the world was introduced to the marvelous era of jet engines, with speed that reduced travel time and technology designed to withstand all types of weather. Douglas Company had a DC-8 with a powerful Pratt & Whitney turbo-jet engine. Their rival, Boeing, came out with the 707, the sleek plane with four turbofan jet engines mounted on its swept wings, a sensation to look at. Its flight deck was every pilot's dream. The console had modern technology. It had color radar, advanced auto pilot, a cockpit voice recorder (better known as the black box), and an air-conditioned cabin, the dream of every passenger. Boeing's slogan was that you were safer in their airplanes than you were in your car.

The public marveled over the modern airliners and commercial flying soared to an-all time high. Gone were the long hours aboard an airplane that rattled your whole body. And while some of us were saddened to see the old Constellation horse leave, we all welcome progress. With this new technology, however, came a price. When news of a crash hit the media it would strike fear into the hearts of everyone, including me. And while statistics confirm that flying is safer than driving, when a plane comes down it is catastrophic; there are rarely survivors. The lost lives, shattered dreams, those final moments—we can only imagine the horror. There is also the pain and suffering of the loved ones left behind. I'm on my way to meet one such loved one, a mother, who shares with me the agony that she and her family went through over forty years ago.

Darnell Mallory
Route 9 South, New Jersey
February 10, 2001
10:45 a.m.

Taking Route 9 south, I pass through Linden and see the little airport to my left, taking me back to my training in 1976. As I continue south, I think of that December day in 1960; it is the reason I am going to a town called Summit, New Jersey. Sorrow and pain came knocking on the door of a peaceful and humble family when Darnell Mallory, son of William and Annie Lou Mallory and brother of William Mallory Jr., Johnny, and Mordine, became one of the 134 who lost their lives on that dark December morning.

I had asked my friend and co-worker Paul Balash to accompany me on this trip. Paul, who is good with maps, was kind enough to agree to serve as my navigator. Arriving early for our two o'clock appointment, we decided to take a tour of this small and quiet town. Paul and I agreed on how beautiful and clean it was and could easily imagine how it was forty years ago. As we sat in a restaurant, having lunch before meeting the Mallorys, I tried to picture in my mind what Darnell Mallory had looked like. I'd only seen a newspaper photo of him. I thought of his teen years, growing up in Summit. I was brought back to the present when I heard a voice say, "Are you all right, man?" It was my friend Paul, who commented that I was just staring out the window, at nothing.

As we walked up the steps to the Mallorys' modest house, I stopped to look around in admiration of the community in which they lived. William Mallory Jr. greeted us at the door and I introduced us as he motioned for us to come in. His father was sitting in a reclining chair watching a football game on TV, his mother was sitting across from the man she married sixty years ago. Entering the house, the first thing I noticed was an oil painting hanging above the fireplace; it was of Darnell, in his basketball uniform. It had been given to the family by a young boy who attended the Baptist church Darnell once attended with his parents and girlfriend Shirley Dean. I felt as if I were taking a step back into the past. I was shown a picture of Darnell taken weeks before his twentieth birthday and a month before his tragic death. You could tell from the picture that he had been full of life and happiness.

Back in 1960, William Mallory Jr. was a freshman at the University Wichita. He and Darnell were very active in sports. William was looking forward to seeing his brother on that day. They had a lot of catching up to do and they had made plans to fly back to school together after the New Year. His parents vividly remember that day, and as they sat there telling their story, you could see the pain in their eyes. At one point, we paused when William Jr. broke down. Even after forty years, the sadness could be overwhelming, and by the end of the interview, which lasted for only an hour, I shared a measure of their grief.

On my way back home to Connecticut, I kept thinking of the interview. I was angered by something William Jr. had told me: His lawyer a trusted friend had taken advantage of them and embezzled some of the money they received as settlement for their son's death. I was also disturbed that United Airlines did not contact the family when the plane went down on that dreadful day, December 16, 1960. Like most of the nation, they learned about the crash from the news media. It was the worst air disaster in American history.

As I had so often ever since that dreadful day, my mind raced back and wondered why it happened. I present here the days leading up to the collision, a port of the lives of seven individuals whose paths crossed each other and became a part of history.

This is not a love story. It has no romantic scenes and there is no happy ending. It is a true story, full of grief, sorrow, courage, and, to this day, unanswered questions. These are true events leading to that devastating day of December 16, 1960.

Ray Garcia
New York City
Lower East Side, Manhattan
December 1960

One windy and cold morning, I woke up to find a thin blanket of snow had covered the entire city throughout the night. Although it wasn't winter yet, New York had been hit with two major storms, setting a trend for what would become a nasty winter. I could never accustom myself to the cold. My parents and I came from Puerto Rico in the early 1950s. We settled in a place called El Barrio up on 106th Street, which we called a home away from home. If you were a Puerto Rican coming to New York, chances were you were headed to El Barrio; ever since the early 1920s it has been home to Puerto Ricans migrating to the United States in search of work. The Barrio extends from 103rd Street up to 116th Street, across Third and Madison Avenues. It is famous for La Marketa, where anything that we might desire from Puerto Rico is sold: garbanzos, yautias, lechon, recao, sofrito, to name just a few of our island products. Every Saturday, it is full of shoppers.

La Marketa officially opened in 1901 to accommodate for the growing number of immigrants. Centered on Third Avenue, it is a long tube from the outside that starts at 116th Street and extends to 103rd Street. Inside there are small shops, each selling its specialty products; some prepare foods to eat there; others offer food to cook at home. You can also buy clothes, sneakers, shoes, and, occasionally, toys. The streets are also packed with sidewalk vendors selling their merchandise. Today La Marketa is not only for Puerto Ricans but for Columbians, Mexicans, and Asians. 116th Street is called the Luis Muniz Marin Boulevard, a tribute to one of Puerto Rico's finest governors.

It was difficult for Puerto Ricans to find work. We brought with us all types of skills, but the English language made life difficult, especially for the elderly, who had to work in an environment they didn't understand and couldn't communicate in. I remember living in a basement (the Dungeon, as I later called it), staying there alone while my parents went to work in a factory for minimum wages. The place was a nightmare.

Later that year, a fire broke out in our building. Thank God for our neighbors above, who alerted us. When it was all over, we were left with nothing. Everything that my parents had worked so hard for was now gone. I recall seeing my mother cry, as my father helplessly looked on. The community church rallied around us, helped my parents fill out some forms, and relocated us to the Lower East Side of Manhattan. My parents were petrified about moving to a place they didn't know, a place with no friends. How would they manage?

But we did move, to a tall building called Jacob Riis Housing at about Sixth Street and Avenue D. The place was beautiful, exquisite, and very neat. There were two elevators and we lived on the twelfth floor, Apt.12E. We finally had our own bathroom and I even had my very own room. It was heaven to me. I had never been in an elevator, nor had I ever been this elevated in my life. My parents were scared that I might fall out the window, but the view was spectacular. I could see the boats crossing the East River. I could also see the East River Park and the highway called the FDR Drive, named for President Franklin D. Roosevelt. It was great. Everybody was warm and kind.

I walked around with my father and tried to observe everything in sight. I could see men playing dominoes outside the little social club they belonged to. Some kids played stickball while others played a rougher game called dodgeball There were grocery stores that catered to our Hispanic culture, which we called bodegas. My favorite spot was the man on the corner selling piraguas, a Spanish term for flavored ice: The man scraped a block of ice with a tool, put the crushed ice into a cup, and added syrup. The syrups came in all different colored bottles, each one a different flavor. My favorite was tamarindo. Another beloved spot was on the corner of Sixth Street where an old Jewish man sold the best potato patties, or knishes, in town. He would arrive early every day in the summer and station himself at that corner until he sold out, and at fifteen cents apiece that didn't take very long. He was well known and respected. Legend has it that he put his two daughters through college, one becoming a lawyer and the other a doctor, just by selling his knishes. Imagine that only in America.

The following year, in November 1960, I turned fifteen. We owned a '52 Plymouth, and Dad had become an owner of a grocery store on Avenue C. The hours were long for both Mom and Dad. I would help out when not attending school. Dad had promised to buy me a Schwinn bike for Christmas. The 1960s were a controversial time. The war in Vietnam was just starting to escalate, which brought out the anger in America, especially its youth. Marijuana and music provided ways to protest the war, and both also allowed young people to escape the discomfort of, and disappointment in, the real world. Young men from all walks of life were being called to serve their country. They were children, too young or too immature to understand what they were getting into and why. The draft was challenged and a domestic war broke out in America. Protesters across the nation defied the law, burning flags in protest. It was an increasingly scary situation. The nation elected a new president, one who promised to lead us into the future.

My best friend and next-door neighbor, Joaquin Pinella, had told me of a place in Brooklyn where there were hundreds of Schwinn bikes on display. Joaquin was born with poliomyelitis. I actually met him in the elevator the day we were moving into our apartment. He showed me around the neighborhood and we quickly became friends. One night, I saw Joaquin in the back of our building, crying, and I asked him what was wrong. I thought he had fallen down, because he was always losing his balance. With his eyes full of tears he said, you're my only friend. Nobody loves me, not even my father. He's ashamed of me. I don't get invited to parties, the kids in school laugh at me, and I'm fourteen and I have never kissed a girl. I wish I was never born. I gave him a hug and promised him that he would always be my best friend. I also told him that people did love him, but he didn't listen.

He blamed God for his circumstance, and hated everyone, including me. One day he took something and overdosed, and he was never the same again. Witnesses who saw him that day stated that just before he collapsed he was screaming up and down the streets, drunk, saying that God had promised him legs; all he had to do was to swallow the pills in his hand. And so he did. The following morning, an ambulance was parked in front of the building where we lived. They were coming for Joaquin. I ran to the hallway to say something to him. I didn't want him to leave. They were bringing him out, strapped into a wheelchair. I cried out his name, but he didn't recognize me or my voice. He just sat there, head bowed. A white sheet covered his body; all you could see was his face. He looked like an old man. He was put into the elevator; I tried to get in but they wouldn't let me. He was only fourteen.

I never saw him again. He was my best friend. I never got to tell him those words. I still think of him, and will always love him.

On December 16, I decided to play hooky from school and go to Brooklyn in search of my bike. Joaquin had given me this address, which he said he got from a newspaper. According to him there were hundreds of bikes on display. The name Schwinn to a kid was like the name Cadillac to an adult. The Schwinn was a wonderful bike; it had chrome fenders, white wall tires, and a cushion spring in front, resembling a shock absorber. The Schwinn was not only for kids, it also was a big hit with the adults. I would see them in the summer riding their bikes in the park, with their girlfriends on the bar close to them as they talked and giggled. The bike was decorated with raccoon tails hanging from each side of the handle bar, a shining chrome headlight, which, when turned on at night, made the bike look even prettier. It was so cool. I had saved money and had already bought the raccoon tails and headlight from a store called Strauss on Fourteenth Street. Now all I needed was the bike. I had already decided on the color of the frame candy apple red and I could picture myself riding it. I really wanted that bike, even if it meant playing hooky from school. And who would know?

Joseph Colacano
Brooklyn, New York
Wednesday, December 14, 1960
7:20 p.m., EST

The streets of Brooklyn were quiet as occupants of this small community cuddled inside their brownstone apartments, avoiding the cold gripping New York. Pedestrians huddled to stay warm from the shifting winds that pummeled their faces, accelerating to their destinations. The streets were illuminated by tall lamp poles that stood guard at every corner like foot soldiers guarding their territory. The reflections from the lights showed the crystal glitter of the light snow coming down from above, gently making contact with the pavement below. Joseph Colacano was desperately searching his apartment for his uncle John's phone number. His uncle's words kept repeating in his mind: "Here's my phone number, Joey. It's the millionth time I've given it to you. Don't lose it!"

Joseph needed to tell John that everything was on schedule for Friday morning. Looking through his wallet, he kept grumbling to himself in anger. He was always losing numbers, and he could never memorize them. If he didn't find this number he would have to make the sixteen-mile trip to Massapequa, Long Island, where John lived. Growing up together in the Brooklyn section of New York, John Oppersiano and Joseph were perhaps as close as an uncle and nephew could be. When Joseph was a toddler, John would help his sister warm up the milk or getting the cloth diapers that were delivered weekly to her home from a laundry company that catered to families with infants. Being only six years apart, John and Joseph were inseparable. They went to the same school together, went to the movies, and watched baseball together. They cried together when, in 1951, the Brooklyn

Dodgers lost the pennant to the New York Giants, when Scotland-born Robert Bobby Thomson hit a humongous home run off Dodgers pitcher Ralph Branca in the ninth inning, stealing the pennant from the Dodgers in a remarkable finish. They still talked and argued with anyone who would listen about how the Giants had stolen the pennant by stealing signals from the Dodgers pitcher. They were even altar boys in the same community church. Being older, John was always looking after his nephew, and at times getting him out of trouble in school.

In the late 1940s, Park Slope, Brooklyn, was mainly populated with Italians and Orthodox Jews, a quiet place to live in. Like every other neighborhood, Park Slope had its parks, where families could go for a stroll on summer days or watch their sons play in the little leagues. Brooklyn was also home of Coney Island and its famous boardwalk, where love bloomed and engagements were proposed. Nathan's hot dogs and the ferris wheel were also main attractions. The community was peaceful and everyone knew each other's children and watched over them like their own. At an early age, John had displayed a flare for business. As a youngster, he would go around his community and collect empty bottles and cans, which he would cash in for money. He was street smart and knew how to negotiate with people much older than he was. He would dazzle them with his speech until he had convinced them. He was always making a quick buck, and always included his nephew in his profits. Like an accountant, John always kept a ledger in which he recorded how much money he had on any given day. His ledger was his bible. If you asked John how much money he had, he would open his book, take stock, and tell you exactly how many nickels, dimes, pennies, and dollars he possessed. John was also a penny-pincher and didn't believe in spending money foolishly. Joseph, on the other hand, was blessed with something else; he was strong, gifted with strength at an early age. He was obsessed with exercise, doing up to two hundred push-ups per day. He admired Steve Reeves, the handsome and mighty warrior, who captured millions of admirers with his movies as Hercules. Steve Reeves had the body that men wanted and Joseph was no exception. Unlike John, Joseph didn't keep a ledger. His money, whenever he had some, was always where he wanted it—in his pocket. In school, he was on the wrestling team. (Rumor has it that when he was only nineteen, he defeated an arm-wrestling champion in Coney Island, breaking the man's wrist.) Everywhere you saw John, you would see Joe. They were always coming up with new plans for making an honest dollar. They sold newspapers on the street corner, or helped a neighbor paint their apartment. They always kept busy, making an honest buck. Half of the money they earned went straight to help their families. They would talk about how one day they would go into business for themselves. They would sit on the stoop of their apartment building and dream of someday having a house, a nice lawn filled with flowers, some kids, a pretty wife, and a new car in the driveway. John's father was the financial adviser. He would talk to the two boys for hours, telling them in his Italian accent, "Boys, this is America. If you study, work hard, and are honest with others, you can get anything you want."

John and Joe promised each other equal partnership in anything they did. Raised in a Catholic environment and having been altar boys, the two were well known in the community. When they reached adulthood, John remained in Brooklyn and Joseph moved to Long Island. They always kept in touch, always talking about a new business, a new venture. One day in December while working his regular job, John came up with a brilliant idea. He realized that he had never seen anyone sell Christmas trees in his community. The idea seemed right, why not sell Christmas trees? It would be for only a few days in the holiday season. John estimated that on his block alone there were at least two hundred families, and most of them bought trees for Christmas. He also knew that he and Joe were well known in the area. It was a great idea, one that couldn't miss. Now all he had to do was call a tree farm, and see how much it would cost to buy them wholesale. He called Joseph, who agreed it was a good idea and said that since his neighbor worked part time on a tree farm in New Jersey, he could get prices. Joseph was desperately looking for John's number when the phone rang. He raced to the phone and was relieved to hear John's exasperated voice at the other end say, "Joe, when the hell were you going to call me?"

"John, thank God, it's you. I've been looking for your number. I know, I know, this is the millionth time you've given it to me."

John interrupted, saying, "Joseph, my dear nephew, remind me to get you a tattoo of my number on your forearm for Christmas. That way you won't lose it."

Joseph told John that he could get all the trees they wanted at two dollars apiece. John had figured that they could sell about three hundred trees that holiday season, but they had to start on Friday. If they sold each tree for seven dollars, they would make a profit of $1,500. John had already talked to a friend of his, the landlord of an unoccupied building that had burned the year before which the boys had helped him clean up. The landlord gave him permission to set up shop for this little venture at no cost. It was a way for the landlord to repay the boys for their help. John instructed Joseph to order only fifty trees at first, to see how it would go, and worked on renting a panel truck to haul the trees from New Jersey back to Brooklyn; they had less than thirty-four hours to put this plan together. John knew they might be ticketed for selling without a peddler's license, but he was hoping that the police officer on the beat would overlook that in the spirit of Christmas. Joseph, excited about the new idea, was already planning what he would do with his share of the money. John warned him not to get his hopes up, but Joseph replied, John, everything you touch turns to gold.

John told his nephew to bundle up on Friday, as it was going to be a cold day, and warned him that he had to be in his house by 4:00 a.m. They would have to be on the street for about eighteen hours, from dawn to dusk, for the next nine days. Joseph replied, "John, you might be the brains, but I'm the strong one. Don't worry, I'll be there. Have I ever let you down?"

John laughed and said, "See you on Friday, tough guy, bright and early."

"Like I said, John, nothing can bring Joey down. As long as we're together, you and me, we're invincible."

"Good night, Joey."

"Good night, Uncle John."

After hanging up with his nephew, John went to the bedroom window and looked out. The streets were empty; the cold weather had kept everyone indoors. He went into his closet to drag out the old boots he had had for over two years and laid them next to his bed, remembering to set the alarm clock for three in the morning. He went to the kitchen to serve himself a cup of black coffee. Sitting there all by himself, he took a pencil and a piece of paper and started to make a profit ledger. He wanted to keep everything in order. That was his job, the rest would come easy. Meanwhile, back in Brooklyn, Joseph was also busy getting ready for the big day, not just for the adventure of selling trees, but also for being with John, his best friend and uncle. He, too, had looked out the window and observed the streets as being very cold and icy. He wanted to make sure he was at Uncle John's doorsteps at precisely four in the morning. As he stared out the window, one thought came to his mind: he had to warm up the car. With the weather being cold, he wanted to make sure his car would start in the-early-morning hours. Then it dawned on him that in all the excitement, he had forgotten to ask John for his phone number.

Steven Baltz
Wilmette, Illinois
Thursday, December 15, 1960
5:30 p.m., CST

Mrs. Pearl Belue, the housekeeper for the Baltz family, had finished her chores and was getting ready to put William Jr. and Steven to bed. William Baltz Sr., vice president and general counsel of the Admiral Corporation of Chicago, was working late that night and had called home to instruct her to put his sons to bed early. Little Stevie had caught a bad cold and sore throat, which had prevented him from traveling to New York with his mother, Phyllis, and nine-year-old sister, Randee, to visit his grandparents in Yonkers. Steven was going to fly alone for the first time and it was a big task to him. He asked Pearl if he could call his mother to find out where she had put the watch he had received for his birthday. He wanted to wear it to show his grandparents. Both Steven and William Jr. attended Wilmette Central, and both were in the Little League and members of the Boy Scouts. Earlier that day, they had attended the school Christmas party, at which Steven was given an award for his dedication and activity in raising money, selling candy for the needy children of his community. The money was to go to the Red Cross for Christmas presents. Pearl allowed Steven to make the call, and, after fifteen minutes on the phone, instructed the young lad to climb into bed. She gave both boys some cough syrup and, as was customary, watched from the entrance to their bedroom as the boys said their prayers. William always said his prayers out loud, Steven kept his private. William's prayer finished with Dear God, protect my brother Steven tomorrow and also protect all those who travel with him, amen.

The Baltz house had been decorated for the Christmas holidays. A six-foot tree stood in the corner of the living room, which Phyliss and her three children had set up before her departure. Presents were scattered around the tree, and it was Pearl's job to keep the boys away from the presents.

After saying her good night to the boys, Pearl returned to the living room to make sure that everything was in order for Steven's early departure to New York. His father was taking him to the airport, where little Stevie would board United 826. Back at the office, William Sr. called Phyllis to tell her that Steven was much improved but that he was still concerned about him traveling alone. Mr. Baltz had considered canceling Steve's trip, but the youngster assured him that he was up to the challenge; Steve was also anxious to see his grandparents, who he hadn't seen in two years. Mr. Baltz wanted his wife to make sure that she was there a little earlier so that his son wouldn't have to wait alone in a city he didn't know. She assured him that was her plan, and that she would call home as soon as Steven arrived.

Mr. Baltz arrived home about nine o'clock that night, took off his coat, and checked the daily mail, which Pearl always left on the kitchen table for him. He then went to his sons' bedroom to check on them. He opened the door a crack to glimpse in at them, then, as he started to close the door, Stevie said, "Hi, Daddy." Mr. Baltz sat on his son's bed and asked him how he was doing. Stevie looked at him and said, "My throat's still a little sore, but I'll be all right once tomorrow gets here."

"Well, you had better get some sleep, son. We both have to be up very early if you want to meet your mother and sister."

Mr. Baltz had never allowed his children to venture out by themselves, especially in an airplane, and this bothered him. Kissing his child on the forehead, William whispered to his son, "Mommy and Daddy love you very much, son. I just want you to know that."

Little Stevie didn't hear those words, for he had fallen asleep.

Darnell Mallory
The University of Omaha (Nebraska)
Thursday, December 15, 1960
6:05 p.m., CST

The score was tied going into the second half of the game as the referee's whistle inside the campus sounded, an indication that half-time intermission was about to begin. Tension was at its best as coaches from both teams discussed strategy with their players, setting their final plans in motion for the final encounter before the Christmas holidays. The visiting team, from the University of Colorado, had already beaten Omaha twice that year, and fans were wondering whether they would do it again. Darnell Mallory, No. 70, was busy getting ready to come in at the second half. His coach had him sit out the first half due to knee injuries he had suffered two weeks earlier against the University of Alabama's mighty team. Playing Alabama was always special to Darnell, who was born there, in a little town called Auburn, on November 14, 1940. The horn sounded as the referee's whistle was heard all around the court, instructing both teams to the middle of the court. Omaha wanted this game. It would be a sweet victory, a Christmas present for their coach. As the whistle blew again the ball was tossed in the air by the official, and both captains reached for the ball. The game was tight throughout the second half, but in overtime Omaha got its first win over Colorado. Darnell had scored twenty points for his team that night. The home crowd went wild, as fans ran from their bleachers onto the court to congratulate their winning team. They actually had two reasons to celebrate: one was winning the basketball game, the other was the start of the Christmas break.

After the game, Darnell headed to his room to start packing for his long-awaited reunion with his family back in Summit, New Jersey. The handsome six-foot-tall athlete had plans to attend the traditional campus Christmas party that night. He had just completed his first three months as a freshman in the university, and the first time he had celebrated his birthday, his twentieth, away from home. He missed his friends, his fiancée, Shirley Dean, and his two brothers and sister, but most of all he missed his mother's cooking and his father's advice. After saying his good-byes to his classmates and teachers, he retired to his room. His plans for that night were to call Shirley and his older sister, Mordine. He had to be up at 4:00 a.m., for the long ride to Chicago where, at 8:45, he would board United 826 for the two-hour flight to New York. His parents would be picking him up. His mother, Annie Lou, was very excited. Her eldest son, William Jr., had already arrived from Kansas, where he attended the University of Wichita, and with Darnell's arrival, it would be the first time in many years that she would have her entire family wake up together on Christmas Day. Darnell's excellent grades and athletic ability at Summit High School had earned him a scholarship to the University of Omaha. He packed his basketball T-shirt, which he had worn to defeat Colorado that night; he planned to give it to his best friend and younger brother, John, on Christmas morning.

After he finished packing, Darnell stopped to look at a newspaper clipping from Alabama that he kept in his scrapbook. It was a reminder of his roots, and the struggle that his parents and grandparents endured in the south. The headline read: Supreme Court Abolishes Bus Segregation. It was only five years earlier, in 1955, that Rosa Parks, with her refusal to give her bus seat to a white man, conveyed the message that blacks had had enough and for many, she was symbolic of the birth of the Civil Rights movement. It took eleven months of boycotting to get justice, but it wasn't over, their biggest fear was retaliation. The system was being upheld with violence, with groups such as the Ku Klux Klan using terrorism to uphold white supremacy. Born just east of Montgomery, Darnell remembered the tension. The Deep South, which included Alabama, Mississippi, Arkansas, and Texas, erupted in racial turbulence, and the segregation of blacks and whites in these states was highly visible all across the country. Darnell remembered living with his grandparents while his parents traveled north to find a better place to raise their four children.

The struggle for civil rights was closely observed by Darnell and it became his ambition, though he loved sports, to enter the political arena.

He wanted to make a difference, to help change the world, and to bring peace among all colors. The events surrounding Rosa Parks and Emmett Till were still fresh in everyone's mind, and even though segregation had been ruled unconstitutional by the Supreme Court in 1956, the white hostility still lingered, even in the North. Every black child, from first graders to college students, feared for their safety. On any given day, they didn't know who was going to strike fear into them, or why.

Darnell's thoughts were interrupted by a knock on the door. It was his friend and teammate, Tom. They were sharing the expense of going to O'Hare Airport, where they were heading home aboard different planes. After saying good night to his friend, Darnell picked up the phone to call Shirley. They spoke for awhile; his last words to her were *Sweet dreams.* He had one more call to make, to his sister, Mordine. Darnell loved his sister; she was the eldest of the four and the wisest. They had a special bond and called each other regularly. Because both their parents worked, Mordine was a surrogate mother in many ways. Called Mother Hen, she was more like the chicken without its head, as she constantly chased the three brothers around the house, trying to discipline them. Mordine told her brother that their parents were picking him up and not to worry if they were a little late, because more bad weather was predicted. As they said their good-byes, Darnell's last words to her were, Tell Mom and Dad that I'll see them tomorrow, and that I love them. Darnell checked his luggage one last time, making sure everything was in order, stashed his plane ticket in his coat pocket, and tucked himself into bed. He lay for a while looking up at the ceiling, thinking how he feared flying, especially in snowy weather. Suddenly remembering he would be flying in the safest plane built, the modern jet called Douglas; he heaved a sigh of relief, turned to his side, reached for the lights, and turned them off.

Vincent Flood
St. Joseph's Priory
Somerset, Ohio
Thursday, December 15
7:08 p.m., EST

Night had already settled on the priory and darkness surrounded the monastery. Looking out the window, all you could see was a halo of snow wrapped around the trees, glittering under the moon above. The view was refreshing to look at and today was a special day for all of the brothers. It was their last supper before leaving the priory to celebrate the Christmas holiday with their families. But for one, it was the last day in the monastery. Vincent De-Paul Flood was sitting quietly in his room, illuminated by a tiny light, signing his letter of resignation. In August, at age nineteen, he had decided to join St. Joseph's Priory in Somerset, Ohio, to follow in his brother's footsteps in becoming a priest. His resignation didn't come easy. Being one of thirteen children born to Mr. and Mrs. Patrick Flood, Vincent knew that it would be difficult for the family, which already had four nuns and one priest, to understand. But Vincent missed his community, and confusion and loneliness had eventually gotten the best of him. He prayed to God for forgiveness and decided to resign.

The novitiate is a year of nonacademic focus, intense in spiritual formation in religious life, where the novices like Vincent learn about the vows of poverty, chastity, and obedience and are trained to become servants of God. At the end of the year, if the novice feels he wants to continue this way of life, he must then petition the church and take a three-year stay in the ministry, after which he becomes a priest. In his diary, which he had begun when he first entered the priory, Vincent wrote:

I haven't seen my family back home, in South Orange, New
Jersey since August. Like every other brother, I too am happy for
tomorrow to arrive, but I'm also saddened. I am very anxious to
meet my friends whom I left behind, wondering how their reaction
would be upon seeing me. Would they think of me as a failure or
a confused friend? And what about my four sisters and brothers
who applauded my decision to become a priest? Would they still
love me? I've come to this conclusion . . . Hoping it's the right
one, while my heart says that I should go forward, I feel that by
doing so I would be lying not only to myself, but also to all those
who put in me not only their faith, but also their trust.

News of his departure spread throughout the monastery. His friends
and brothers, all twenty-eight of them, were saddened but no one dared
to advise him. That was standard policy only with the help of God could
Vincent make such a difficult decision but emotions and sorrow were highly
visible. Believing he had failed his community as well as his family, Vincent
was, in his heart, nevertheless convinced that it was the right decision. He
had prepared a statement to read to his priory brothers at the last supper
that he would have with them. He wanted to tell them why he had chosen
to leave the monastery, and to thank them for their kind ways toward him.
Still in jeans, Vincent hurried to prepare himself for the wonderful gathering.
He had time to call his home back in New Jersey to tell his family that he
was chosen to say grace. He was nervous and wanted advice from his older
brother Kevin, who had gone through the same studies several years before
him. With his heart beating as he dialed the number to his home, Vincent
waited as the phone rang. Suddenly a voice came, Happy Holidays! This is
the Flood residence. It was his father, Patrick.

"Dad, it's Vincent. Happy holidays to you, too."

"Vincent, how are you, son? Your mother and I were just talking about
you."

"Dad, you'll never believe it. I've been chosen to give grace."

"That's wonderful, son. Hold on . . . Kevin, your brother is giving grace
at the priory tonight."

Kevin took the phone. The sound of his voice came on with joy for
his younger brother. "Vincent," said Kevin, "how happy I am for you! You
know, I was chosen to give grace on one such occasion, Thanksgiving, but
to give grace on the most celebrated holiday, that's an honor, dear brother.
We're all proud of you."

"Kevin, how are Mom and Dad taking it?"

"What do you mean?" replied Kevin.

"You know, me leaving the ministry."

"Vincent, we all here love you dearly, and we respect your decision."

There was silence for a moment and Kevin could hear Vincent weeping as he tried not to let his emotions take over. "Vincent," he said, "are you all right?"

"Yes, brother, it's just that I wanted very much for you to be proud of me. I wanted to share and feel what you feel as a priest, and now that won't happen."

Vincent's weeping turned into crying. Deep down inside, he was hurt and confused, but he knew that at the age of nineteen, being a priest would mean sacrifice, something he wasn't prepared to do. Kevin allowed his brother to let out his emotions before continuing his conversation.

"Listen, Vincent, just concentrate on tomorrow. When you're here, we'll talk, all right? Listen, Mom wants to talk to you. Don't worry. Everything is going to be all right, I promise you."

Vincent's mother took the phone. "How's my baby?"

"Mom, how I miss you."

"Vincent, why are you crying?"

"Mom, it's just that I wanted to do this with all my heart, but now it seems as if Satan has won."

"Don't say that, son. Your heart is still in the right place. So you won't be a priest, but you can be a lawyer or doctor. You know we do need a doctor in the family."

She knew her son was in pain and wished she could be with him to comfort him, but he was a long way from New Jersey. She assured him that he was loved, and that nothing would change that.

After saying his good-byes, Vincent rushed to change clothes. He wanted to be at the dining hall earlier than the others in order to practice his speech. His mentor and novice-master, Father Ferrer Cassidy, entered the room as Vincent was rehearsing his speech and interrupted with warm applause. Embarrassed, Vincent stopped. The priest, amused by it all, walked over to his pupil, put his arm around him, and said, "Brother Lawrence, don't worry. You're among friends and fellow brothers. Here's a word of advice: make it short, make it meaningful." With that, Vincent breathed a sigh of relief. Within fifteen minutes, the hall was full with fellow priests and novices, the mass was about to get started, and everyone was seated at their assigned place. All eyes were focused on two things: the food, and Brother Lawrence.

Finishing his prayers, Brother Lawrence thanked everyone for their patience with him and wished everyone a safe trip home. A special prayer was said by Father Cassidy, blessing all of his pupils for a safe return to his monastery, the house of God. After having dinner, Vincent went to his room and reached under his bed to retrieve a package, a Christmas present for Father Cassidy. Walking the long corridor to the chapel, he stood a moment and stared at the crucifix. Approaching the altar, he went up to the cross and kissed the feet of Jesus, saying, with tears in his eyes, "I'm sorry." Father Cassidy's office was a couple of doors down. Vincent knocked and heard Father Cassidy's voice tell him to enter. Nervous as always, Vincent entered. Extending his arm, he handed his gift to the priest, saying, "Merry Christmas."

The novice master leaned over and hugged the young apprentice, kissing him on the cheek.

"Open it, Father."

The priest, thrilled by the package, tore off the wrapping paper. It was a red scarf. The high priest immediately wrapped it around his neck as he walked around his office in pride.

"Vincent," Father Cassidy said, "every time I wear this, I will always think of you and this day. Thank you, my son."

That night, Vincent went back to his room, knowing that he had done the right thing. He called his house again to tell his family about his night with his brothers. Kevin told him with a happy voice that they were all proud of him. They were waiting for him with open arms.

"Kevin, how's the weather there, 'cause it's awful here. Do you think they might cancel the flight?"

"Well, it's pretty bad here too, but God will be watching over you and all of the passengers with you. Tomorrow will be a divine day, just for you."

With that Vincent said good-bye again and hung up. He went to his closet and neatly placed his clothes that he was going to wear the following day. He kneeled alongside his bed, looking up at the crucifix that hung on the wall next to his bed, and prayed to God for a safe trip for all.

"Dear God, I'm so scared and I guess I don't have to tell you that, 'cause you know everything that I think of. As I leave tomorrow, please understand that I'm only human, and though you have given me strength and wisdom to think for myself, it is you who I look to for advice. Please try to understand that while my love for you will never diminish, I am not the one to carry your message dressed in black, but I do promise this to you here and now, that I will never abandon your voice. Please tell me that Satan hasn't won, for I feel that he has tonight."

His prayers were interrupted by a knock on the door. It was Brother John, who, like Vincent, was leaving the ministry. They had both joined the priory in August, and both were flying back to their homes. A taxi was driving them to the airport and he stopped in to remind Vincent to be ready by 6:00 a.m. John, who was flying to Colorado aboard Pan Am, had always feared flying and told Vincent he preferred to drive to Colorado, but the weather was too much for him to handle by himself. Vincent assured him that flying was safer than driving, but admitted that he too was a little scared of flying. John suddenly blurted out, "Vincent, what if God is mad at us and punishes us?"

Vincent, with a look of fear on his face, said, "What do you mean?"

"Suppose, he brings down our plane in anger?"

Vincent looked at him and said, "John, God doesn't work that way. He would never do that to his children, especially on Christmas."

John looked at Vincent, then at the crucifix on the wall. He gave Vincent a strong hug and walked out.

Los Angeles Airport
United Airlines, Terminal A
Friday, December 16
2:45 a.m., PST

Captain Robert Sawyer had been hired by United Airlines in January 1941. He held a valid airman certificate with a current airline transport certificate, # 70677. His rating included DC-3, B-247, DC-4, DC-6, and now DC-8. He had a total of 19,100 flying hours, of which 344 were in DC-8s. He had qualified in the DC-8 on June 6, 1960. He was current on proficiency checks and route qualification. His last medical examination had been in September 1960. First Officer Robert W. Fiebing, was employed by United Airlines in May 1951. He held a current airline transport certificate, # 439262. His rating included DC-3, DC-4, DC-6, DC-7, and DC-8 aircraft.

First Officer Robert W. Fiebing had a total of eighty-four hundred hours, of which 416 were in the DC-8. He had been rated on the DC-8 in May 1960. His last medical had been in August 1960.

Second Officer Richard E. Prewitt, the flight engineer, was hired by United Airlines in September 1955. He had an airline transport certificate, # 1161137, and flight engineer certificate # 1329809. His ratings included DC-6, DC-7, and DC-8 aircraft. Second Officer Prewitt, who had just turned thirty, had a total of eighty-five hundred hours of flying time, of which 379 were as flight engineer in the DC-8. His most recent medical checkup had been in August 1960.

Combined, these men had logged a total of thirty-six thousand hours of flight time, over eleven hundred of which were in a DC-8.

An early morning breeze fanned the tarmac of the airport, but the humidity was already settling in. For the past five days, California had been suffering from a heat wave and the forecast was for more of the same. California was a popular destination for the holidays and this Christmas season was one of the busiest. The airport had flights coming in day and night, a nonstop operation, as people from all walks of life descended on Los Angeles for some vacation pleasure. At 2:00 a.m., however, the airport had finally quieted down. The cleaning crews came out to prepare for the morning rush and for a while, the only sounds you could hear were from the vacuum cleaners and floor buffers.

The first flight to leave that morning was United 856, an empty flight to Chicago's O'Hare Airport, where it would pick up passengers and crew members and its flight number would change to 826 for its final destination, Idlewild International Airport in New York City. The DC-8 was parked at Terminal A, Gate 8. A glitter of white rained over the sleek jet, a reflection of the full moon that was setting over Los Angeles. The plane's crew of three was already making preparations for the first leg of the trip, scheduled to depart at 3:00 a.m. They each had their assignments and knew their jobs. Captain Sawyer was busy doing his preflight inspection of the DC-8. While reviewing his checklist, he thought about his first time in the air. He was only sixteen years old, and was helping a friend and pilot build a monoplane, which later they flew. Ever since, Captain Sawyer knew he belonged in the air. That was over thirty years ago, and now he was a captain for a major airline, commanding a brand new fifty-million-dollar jet. The thought brought a smile to his face. He reached into his shirt pocket to get a pen, and felt a piece of paper tucked inside. It was a Christmas list that his wife, Patricia, had given him. His last leg would take him into New York for a couple of days, where he was to buy Christmas presents for his three daughters. His friend and copilot, First Officer Fiebing, who was upstairs in flight operations with a meteorologist plotting their course to Chicago, and flight engineer Second Officer Prewitt all planned to go together to Macy's in Manhattan for a day of shopping.

Californian all his life, Fiebing didn't like winter weather and operations had just informed him that a heavy snowfall had hit the entire eastern coast. Chicago was practically snowed in, and flight operations and ground crews were working to open in time for the morning rush. New York had also been hit and was put on weather alert. Meteorologists advised Fiebing to expect to hit the white stuff in Colorado, which meant that the flight would encounter turbulence until touchdown in New York. Captain Sawyer finished his walk around the jet a while and was joined by Fiebing as he got ready to board, while Prewitt, who was already inside the cockpit, was going through his checklist.

Prewitt's job was to keep the aircraft in good mechanical working order, a job he was well qualified to do. It seemed Prewitt could fix anything put before him, which had earned him the nickname Mr. Fix-It. The trio had been flying together for the last six months, and all three had been certified and promoted to the DC-8. The crew was flying empty, and the captain liked it that way, peaceful and quiet.

"United 856, this is Los Angeles ground control, you're clear to start engines, 1, 2, 3, and 4, over."

"Roger, replied the first officer. Clear to start all four engines."

The airport was awakened by the sound of the four huge Pratt & Whitney engines coming to life, the sound escalating as the captain revved up the RPMs. The crew was busy going through their checklists, turning switches on, lighting up the plane as they completed their checklists. You could see the reflections of the strobe lights from the tip of each wing lighting the dark tarmac floor as the red rotating beacon swept the entire area. The motor man linked his small but powerful tow truck to the nose of the plane and slowly towed it away from the terminal. Sitting back and enjoying the ride as the truck towed them into position, the crew joked about the weather, and how the cold weather was going to wipe the tans off their faces. The motor man signaled that they were clear and drove away, leaving the jet to taxi on its own.

"Los Angeles ground, this is United 856. Ready when you are."

"Roger, United, you're cleared to taxi to runway two, winds two three zero degrees at five miles per hour, altimeter 29.30 and holding steady. Temperature 76 degrees, contact departure control on frequency 121.9. Good day."

"Roger ground. Contact departure control on 121.9. Good day."

The DC-8 jet slowly taxied to its active runway, awaiting clearance for takeoff. As always, the three crew members placed their hands on top of each other's before takeoff, a ritual they started when they had teamed up six months earlier. To them, it meant honor and respect, as well as good luck. The captain would have the last word, saying, "Gentleman, let's get this show on the road."

Just then the intercom came on. It was LA departure control.

"United 856 this is Los Angeles departure. Sir, you're cleared for takeoff, Merry Christmas and safe journey."

"Roger departure control, Merry Christmas to all, and thank you. United 856 is now rolling."

The captain placed his right hand on the throttle and pushed forward, the sound of the mighty engines roaring with power as the jet steadied, maintaining its course on the active runway, following the broken white line in the middle of the runway as the jet approached V1, the first marker of velocity on approach. Seconds later, the first officer called out V2. The captain acknowledged as he pulled back on the yoke, lifting the nose of the plane to a thirty-degree angle. The plane lifted from the tarmac, and slowly disappeared into darkness.

TWA Flight 266
Inbound
Port Columbus Airport
Friday, December 16
5:51 a.m.

Captain David A Wollam, age thirty-nine, was employed by TWA on May 23, 1945. He held a valid airman certificate with currently effective airline transport certificate, # 261640. He had logged more than fourteen thousand hours of flight time, and had flown everything from the DC-3 to the Marlin 202 and 404 series. He was certified to fly the four-propeller planes in September 1952, and he had a total of 252 hours in the old Constellation. He was current in the requirements of proficiency checklines, check-route qualifications, and recurrent training. His last federal aviation medical check-up had been on October 31, 1960.

First Officer Dean T. Bowen, age thirty-two, was employed by TWA in July 1953. He held a current airline transport certificate and was rated in the Lockheed Constellation aircraft. He had a total of six thousand hours, of which 268 were in the Constellation. He qualified on this type of equipment in May 1959. His best friend and classmate, Le-Roy Rosenthal, age thirty, was employed by the airline in May 1956 and had a total of thirty-five hundred hours as a flight engineer, two hundred of which were in the Constellation. He, too, was picked to move up the ladder to the jet era.

Security was tight in Port Columbus Airport as Air Force Two touched down with newly elected Vice President Lyndon B. Johnson aboard. The white-and-blue Boeing 707 landed at runway 5, where it remained with the vice president while highly visible Secret Service men literally shut the airport down. Within minutes, the plane was surrounded by men in uniform with their weapons in arms. A sleek black Lincoln limousine with flags on both sides and the vice-presidential seal on the door rolled alongside Air Force Two. Johnson and his wife, Lady Bird, had attended a funeral the previous night for a dear friend of theirs and they were making a stopover in Ohio on their way back to Washington. The passengers in the terminal were excited that the vice president was in town. Everyone was trying to get a glimpse of the couple, and the Secret Service was scrambling to secure all doors leading to the tarmac, where the plane waited.

In the meanwhile, five thousand feet above in the morning darkness, planes were being stacked up to accommodate Air Force Two. Port Columbus Tower was advising traffic that there would be a forty-five-minute delay. TWA 266 was number three in the stacking order. Captain David A. Wollam was the man in command of the Constellation plane. He and his crew, First Officer Dean T. Bowen and Flight Engineer Le-Roy L. Rosenthal, had departed the Dayton airport two hours earlier and they were landing at Port Columbus for a two-hour layover to pick up additional passengers and fly them to LaGuardia Airport in New York. Because they flew on a weekly basis, most of the passengers were familiar executives from different companies that had contracts with TWA. Captain Wollam was coming down with the flu and was much in need of rest. His 4:00 a.m. walk-around inspection of the ten-year-old Constellation had made it worse. He was anxious to get home to his family in Little Neck, Long Island, where he would have a three-day rest before returning to duty.

The tower came on as they were clearing Air Force Two for takeoff. The TWA crew made a sound of relief, as Captain Wollam instructed his First Officer Bowen to review the landing checklist and Flight Engineer Rosenthal busied himself with last-minute preparations. The stewardesses made sure all passengers were buckled in when the Fasten Seat Belts sign flashed on. Patricia Post, age twenty, was the youngest stewardess on board. She had lived with her mother, Elvira, until she graduated at the University of Pennsylvania in 1959 and moved to a small apartment in Jackson Heights in Queens, New York. Despite working with the airline for only ten months, she was notified via telegram given to her by the company's personnel officer in Dayton that she was one of the twenty stewardesses chosen to fly TWA newest fleet of jets. The telegram stated that this would be her last flight on a Constellation before going into training in January 1961. Her friend and fellow stewardess,

Margaret Gernat, who had been flying for the airline since 1958, had also been promoted to the jet era. Both were ecstatic.

"TWA 266, this is Port Columbus approach. You're number three to land, runway five, winds fifteen gusting to twenty-five at one hundred degrees, temperature is twenty-two degrees. You're to follow Pan Am 707 on down wind leg. Do you have traffic in sight? over."

"Columbus this is TWA 266 negative on the bird. It's pretty bad up here. Can you guide? over."

"TWA 266, roger that. This is Columbus, how's visibility up there? over."

"Columbus, we have some wet snow coming down, making it difficult to see, and the winds are kicking the hell out of us. It's also awfully dark. over."

"Roger, TWA squawk transponder on 121.0. over."

"TWA squawking at 121.0."

"TWA, Columbus has you on radar. Pan Am is now turning base. Can you confirm?"

"Roger, Columbus. TWA, we have traffic in sight."

"Roger TWA, please stand by, gentlemen."

As the captain called out for more flaps, the plane hit unexpected turbulence, making everyone a little jittery. The plane didn't handle too well under turbulence, becoming sluggish and heavy. Seated in her seat, Patricia looked at Margaret and said with a nervous smile, "Gee, Margaret, imagine if after getting promoted, this old heap crashes on our last day."

Margaret returned her nervous smile, and said, "No way, Pat, we're going to the academy, and we're going to be stewardesses on those new fabulous jets."

As the crew heard the Pan Am jet acknowledge touchdown, the tower came on again. "TWA, this is Columbus. Sorry for the delay, guys. You're cleared to land runway five, conditions remaining the same. TWA 266, you're clear to land, over."

"Roger, Columbus, clear to land TWA 266."

Captain Wollam made a ninety-degree turn to the left, aligning the Constellation on its final approach as the wind tossed the hundred-thousand-pound plane with its four-propeller Wright engines around like a kite. In the cabin, the uneasy passengers held onto the arms of their seats. The ceiling lights of the plane flicked on and off as the crew struggled to keep the plane on its course. They were still ten miles away from landing as the outer marker went on, confirming that they were on the glide slope and on course leading to runway five. The flight engineer was given the task of lookout, to search for the lights that would lead them to the runway. Captain

Wollam and First Officer Bowen tackled the controls. The middle marker horn sounded, but there was still no sign of the runway. Captain Wollam was contemplating a go-around when Flight Engineer Rosenthal suddenly shouted, "Runway at one o'clock!"

"Roger that," said the captain as the ILS strobe lights of the airport came into view.

In his eight years as captain flying the Constellation, Captain Wollman had never encountered such a difficult landing.

"TWA 266, Columbus has you in sight. There's a wind shear alert and caution is advised. You're clear to land, over."

"Roger that, Columbus, thanks for the advice. TWA clear to land."

As the plane touched down, the sigh of relief was audible among the crew, and the passengers and stewardesses broke out in a round of applause for the crew.

Captain Wollam, his face perspiring, told Dean to taxi the old horse into the terminal. Ohio was pretty much snowed in, and the maintenance crew was busy deicing the airplanes that were standing, awaiting takeoff. Just then, Margaret came into the cockpit to congratulate the crew. "Good job, you guys."

The captain leaned back and said, "It's not over yet, Marge. We still have New York to get to."

"Hey, we only have three more hours before I'm cuddled up in my warm and cozy apartment in Queens. What can possibly go wrong?"

Wollam smiled and said, "Lucky you. I have to travel to Little Neck. Hey Marge, isn't your birthday tomorrow?"

"Yeah, how did you know?"

Well, let's just say that I have a knack for remembering dates. Hey guys, did you know that Margaret is a graduated nurse of Bellevue Hospital in Manhattan? Happy birthday, Marge."

United Flight 856
27,000 feet over Council Bluffs, Iowa
Friday, December 16
6:01 a.m.

The rotating beacon swept through the semi-darkened skies over Iowa, a grayish-purple sky outlining the atmosphere as the clouds came into view. Below, the terrain was peaceful. Chunks of snow splattered the DC-8 as it cruised along its route. The windshield wipers were blasting the wet snow from the cockpit's window. Inside, Captain Sawyer was sitting with his first and second officers, sipping hot black coffee. They had been in the air for over two hours and were preparing themselves for what was ahead: snow, shifting winds, and possible wind shear can be undetectable and radical shift in the wind's speed and direction can without warning force a plane, regardless of its size or power, to the ground. The captain and crew were well aware of this phenomenon, which aviation experts were still trying to understand.

For the crew of United 856, the situation was also familiar. The DC-8 was performing well above capacity, leaving the captain worry-free. A small glitch with the second VOR had occurred early into the flight. The receiver had stopped operating for a moment, but it was operational within seconds. Flight Engineer Prewitt suggested that turbulence had caused the needle to freeze out. Other than that, the crew was satisfied with the plane's performance. The DC-8 had been purchased by United the year before and had only a few hundred hours of flight time under its belt. Its most recent inspection had been done in August, and the entry log showed no mechanical deficiencies or structural fatigue. Although the plane was set on autopilot, First Officer Fiebing was manning the controls, monitoring the gauges before him. The pilots took turns flying the aircraft from point A to point B, or what is known as leg flying. The captain usually flew the first and the last legs of a journey, but Sawyer had decided earlier that, weather permitting, he would give Fiebing his opportunity to land the DC-8. He felt his first officer was ready and considered it a sort of holiday present to him.

The responsibilities of a captain commanding a plane safely across open airspace are enormous. Lives depend on him, making every decision a critical one. He trains his co-pilot in proficiency flying, the dos and don'ts, everything from engine failure to aborted takeoffs, so that one day he would be ready to captain his own airship. The goal of any flight engineer is to fly in the right seat, and, eventually, in the left, where the captain sits.

"Davenport uni-com, this is United 856, over your airspace at 27 thou, frequency 122.8 inbound to O'Hare International, over."

"Roger 856, this is Davenport, receiving you in frequency 122.8, over."

"Davenport, United 856, we need vector for O'Hare and weather report, over."

"Roger 856, please set frequency to 118.1, squawk transponder on 121.9 for radar, over."

"Roger that, Davenport, switching to 118.1, squawk 121.9 now, over."

"United 856, Davenport Municipal has you on radar. Stand by."

"Standing by, 856."

The captain was in communication with the tower as the jet approached Davenport. Winds were starting to pick up, occasionally tossing the jet around. The crew could sense that the plane was getting sideswiped from all sides as the snow mixed with the changing wind, which made them a bit tense. The crew had been relying solely on instruments since their departure in the dark; now, with morning, they had to contend with Mother Nature and blinding snow. The morning sun was attempting to break from the clouds that were coming into view the glare made it difficult to see, leaving the crew partially blind. The captain ordered the flight engineer to turn up the heat to get the chill out of the aircraft. They were now in cold weather territory.

"United 856, this is Davenport. Weather report is as follows: winds zero one zero degrees at twenty-two miles per hour, barometer 30.10, surface winds at O'Hare at twenty-seven miles per hour. What are your intentions 856? over."

'Davenport, United 856. We need clearance to 18 thou entering Chicago's airspace, over.'

"Roger, 856, you've been approved for 18 thou, turn left heading zero nine five, vector to Peoria Illinois is PIA 356, over."

"Roger, Davenport, United 856 leaving 27 for 18 vector PIA 356. Good day."

Arthur Swenson
Columbus, Ohio
The Holiday Inn
Friday, December 16
6:11 a.m.

With just a little under three hours before boarding, Arthur Swenson busily prepared his luggage for the flight home. Due to a late conference call to his boss from Pratt & Whitney, where he worked, he had had no time to pack the night before. He had also spent time finalizing the contract that had been awarded to his company by the government just two days earlier. Employed as a project engineer by Pratt & Whitney in 1941, Arthur and his wife and three children had relocated from New Jersey to Glastonbury, Connecticut, for his new assignment. At age forty-two, he considered himself a lucky man he had married his high-school sweetheart, had three beautiful children, and enjoyed his line of work. The idea of traveling made him uneasy. Looking out the hotel window, he noticed it was still dark outside. The parking lot was partly empty as the snow softly struck the pavement; it had been snowing since Wednesday. A Christmas tree glittered at the front door, where the doorman huddled to keep himself warm from the snow, which had been nonstop since Wednesday.

Finishing his luggage, Arthur looked around to make sure he hadn't forgotten anything. As was his custom, he made sure that the bed was made, something he had learned from his parents. Always the professional on business trips, Arthur sat down to and wrote a note in a notebook left by the hotel-cleaning crew. In it, he thanked the hotel for good service and hospitality, and he tucked in five dollars for the maid, who was always attentive to his needs while he stayed there. The idea of being away from home never appealed to him, especially during the Christmas holidays, but it was part of his job and his family was quite supportive of it. Arthur called a cab service three hours before boarding time. He called well in advance because of the poor weather; he wanted to be at Port Columbus Airport by 8:00 a.m. so he could eat breakfast before the 8:45 a.m. boarding for TWA 266 to LaGuardia. He also wanted to call his wife, Virginia. They had arranged for her to pick him up at the airport, but he wanted to tell her not to make the long drive to New York from Glastonbury in the snow.

With the jet era in full blast, Pratt & Whitney was introducing the JT3C-6 turbojet engine, its newest design. Its competitor, Rolls Royce, had its own version, and the two were constantly competing for lucrative government contracts. The United States Armed Forces were looking for new technology for their twenty-year-old planes, and the two companies had excellent products to offer. Pratt & Whitney had locked in contracts with Douglas Company for their new DC-8 jets, which were already popular with several major airlines. As Arthur sat in the hotel lobby waiting for the cab service to pick him up, a smile crossed his face a smile of accomplishment, for his trip had paid off. After all those long hours of working late to make his presentation perfect, this was going to be a good Christmas for him and his family, because he knew that a bonus was coming his way for the extra effort that he put into the project. He figured that since his three children Douglas, Joyce, and Elizabeth were off from school for the holidays, it would be a good time for the family to take a vacation to Florida. He owed it to himself and his family for their patience.

"Mr. Arthur Swenson?"

His thoughts were interrupted by the sound of his name being called. His taxi had just arrived to take him to the airport.

"I'm Arthur Swenson," he replied, raising his hand.

"Hi, Mr. Swenson, I'm Billy, your driver. Let me get the luggage for you, sir."

"Thank you, Billy."

Rising from the chair he had occupied, Art felt something slip from his right hand. He adjusted his reading glasses to look down at the falling object. It was his boarding pass. As he bent to retrieve it, the three red letters TWA stood out in some way he couldn't explain. Feeling strange, he suddenly called to Billy, who was reaching to open the hotel door on his way out.

"Billy," he said, "can you wait a minute? I want to go to the hotel chapel for a minute."

"Sure, Mr. Swenson," Billy replied, "I'll be waiting by my cab."

Art walked over to the hotel clerk, who was just starting her shift, and with a somewhat embarrassed look on his face asked her for directions to the chapel. It wasn't that he was scared he had been around planes all his life; it was the way the ticket fell from his hand that seemed ominous. Entering the empty chapel feeling a bit silly, he looked around him, kneeled at the altar and said a prayer, and walked out.

Port Columbus
Arrival Terminal
Section C, Gate 9
Friday, December 16
6:43 a.m.

The airport coffee lounge was open for business. The aroma of freshly brewed coffee was in the air as passengers gathered around the tables, enjoying their early morning breakfast. Ground crews were busy cleaning the runways and the baggage handlers were loading the luggage into the planes. The blizzard that had begun the previous day gave no sign of letting up. Looking out from the terminal, all you could see was the glitter of the flakes as they fell from above.

Port Columbus Airport, a twenty-four-hour operation with three runways, was struggling to stay open but found it increasingly difficult to do so. All around the tarmac, mechanics and line men were busy preparing planes for departure. Some trucks were filling the aircraft with fuel while others sprayed the planes with chemicals in order to de-ice their wings. Inside the passenger terminal the scene was quite different. There was a certain excitement in the air as people from all walks of life gathered, carrying walk-on luggage in one hand and shopping bags filled with presents in the other. Children were running around as their mothers tried to keep them from wandering away. The weather had brought everyone to the airport much earlier than usual. Most were there for the nine o'clock flight to New York aboard Trans-World Airline 266. The plane had already landed, and while it was being refueled Captain Wollam and his crew took advantage of the two-hour break to relax and to call home. The severity of the storm was apparent from the bulletin board, which showed that flights were being delayed or canceled. It kept the flight operation and tower controllers busy, calculating what to do with each flight, and kept passengers and well-wishers in a state of uncertainty, not knowing whether their flights would actually depart.

Most of Port Columbus departures were heading east to the three busiest airports: Newark in New Jersey, and LaGuardia and Idlewild, both in New York; all were hit hard with snow. Newark, though trying to remain open, had already diverted flights to Idlewild. Everyone wanted snow for Christmas, but not so much of it!

The novice passenger is unaware of how much behind-the-scenes effort goes into air travel, men and women working long hours to ensure that travelers get from point A to point B safely and on time. Pilots do not choose to fly in snowstorms, but it is part of their job and they are well trained for it.

The crew from TWA 266 was gathered in the coffee lounge, waiting for a go-ahead from flight operations. They were all lost in their own thoughts.

"Isn't she beautiful?" Patricia blurted out. Margaret looked around confused. Then Pat pointed to the red and white Constellation and said, "I'm talking about our Connie. Look at her! Isn't she beautiful, with the snow falling on her and the floodlights making her gleam?"

Everyone nodded in agreement. Just then a huge round of applause was heard from the customer service desk. TWA 266 to New York had just been given the green light to depart on time. The crew was advised that the maintenance checks and loading of supplies were completed. It was time to prepare for their final destination.

United Flight 856
Twelve thousand feet over Peoria, Illinois
Friday, December 16
6:49 a.m.

"United 856, this is Chicago's O'Hare airport squawk transponder at 120.7, over."

"Roger, O'Hare, United 856 transponder at 120.7 squawking now, over."

"Roger, 856, Chicago has you on radar, turn heading 087 degrees, clear to descend to 9000, contact approach control at 119.0, over."

"Roger, Chicago, United 856 turning 087 degrees leaving 12 for 9, switching to 119.0."

The crew was happy that they were minutes from touchdown, and not just because of the rough weather that they had encountered, all three were hungry. For the past three hours, they had been drinking only coffee. The morning sun was coming into view. The weather was picking up as they headed east. Although the captain was looking forward to landing, he wasn't too anxious to step off the plane. With all the commotion around him, he had forgotten to pack his black raincoat, so he'd have no protection from the freezing rain they were about to encounter. He reminded himself to drink plenty of tea; he didn't want to catch a cold for the holidays, and he still had four days before heading back to sunny California. The plane was on its cruise descent when First Officer Fiebing noticed something.

"Captain, the second VOR is acting up again."

The captain shifted his attention to his second officer, Richard Prewitt. "Richard, what do you make of it?"

Just then Fiebing interrupted the captain. "I'll be darned, its okay now, Cap. It has to be a frozen connector."

Prewitt replied, "Remind me to get it checked while we're in New York, okay guys? Bobby, contact Chicago."

"Chicago approach control, this is United 856 inbound, frequency 119.0 holding at nine, over."

"Roger, United 856, this is Chicago approach control. We have you on radar, winds 290 degrees at seventeen miles per hour, barometer 31.12, runway in use thirty-two right turn 040 degrees, descent to five. Call me when you reach your assigned altitude, over."

"Roger, Chicago approach, United 856 turn to heading 040, leaving nine for five. We'll call you when we get there, over."

United 856 was on its final descent. The ground below was still not visible and all they could see in front of them was a white blanket of snow mixed with fog. The instruments were all they had to guide them. Inside the cockpit, the crew concentrated on the descent as each man assumed his responsibility in bringing the jet to a safe altitude. Minutes seemed like hours as the plane searched its way toward earth. It had been three hours since they left Los Angeles and they have been flying solely on instrument flight rule, a method based solely on the panel, so the crew depends on the accuracy of their instruments and it had placed a heavy strain on their eyes as well as their bodies. The panel consists of more than twenty gauges and over forty switches, all of them vital. They are used for the artificial horizon, which tells the pilots that their planes are flying straight and level, the turn-and-bank indicator, which enables the plane to bank left or right without stalling, and the gyro compass for navigation. They also include the very-high-frequency omnidirectional radio range, known as VOR technology developed during World War II that enables the pilots of instrument-equipped planes to determine their position more efficiently. (An understanding of the VOR is important, as you will understand its role at the end.)

United 856 was being bounced around as the winds at five thousand feet were starting to pick up. While the empty jet was handling above means, Captain Sawyer didn't want to stay in the altitude assigned to him because he was concerned it would damage his new plane. He knew from experience what weather of this severity can do to a plane. He also knew it was likely the winds would become increasingly violent as they approached the airport. Grabbing the communications mike, Captain Sawyer was about to call Chicago when they came on and said:

"To all aircraft inbound, this is Chicago approach control, please maintain speed and heading. We have an emergency in progress."

Vor Model (King Ki-203) Nav/Comm
Similar to United Flight 826

The crew of the United sat in silence as they awaited further instructions. When an emergency is in progress, aircraft in a holding pattern maintain silence while the tower controllers handle the situation, but Captain Sawyer was about to break that rule. He needed to get away from the winds that were hammering his aircraft and crew. Reaching again for the mike, Captain Sawyer took a deep breath and commenced his transmission.

"Approach control, this is United 856. What's the holdup? over." There was no response.

"Control, I say again this is United 856. What is the holdup? over." Pause.

"United 856, this is approach control, we're going to open a new runway. We have a 707 that skidded off the active runway. We're in the process of removing, over."

"Roger, approach, how many do you have on scope? over."

"856, we have sixteen stacked up. You're number nine to land, over."

"Tower, any chance of leaving five? I'll go up or down, just get us out of five, over."

"United 856, are you requesting emergency assistance? over."

Pause. "Negative approach, but we're bouncing all over at five thousand, we need to leave five, over."

"United 856, this is approach, please say again, your transmission is breaking up, over."

"Approach, United 856, we need to get away from five, we're being bounced around, we need clearance to another altitude, over."

"Roger, United, stand by while I check other traffic for safe passage. over."

"Roger, approach. United standing by. over."

There was no sign that the weather was going to dissipate as the crew waited for the tower to come back on line, so all they could do was wait. There was concern among the crew as they stared out the cockpit window into nothing. A white blanket of fog mixed with wet snow pummeled the jet. There was nothing to see above or below, and Captain Sawyer put the crew on alert; he instructed his second officer to be the lookout man, while his first officer took readings from the instruments.

"United, this is approach control, clear to climb to nine thousand, maintain present heading. Inform when you reach nine, over."

The jet was on a shallow twenty-degree climb and there were specks of holes in the clouds allowing the crew to see land, but with the new altitude assigned to them, they would once again be in the blind. The windshield wipers were turned to maximum; wet snow was making its way to Chicago.

The weather was picking up and it seemed that any altitude wouldn't be safe enough. The crew needed to land the plane. Then, like an answered prayer, a voice came over the intercom.

"United 856, this is approach control. Gentlemen, we're diverting the first eight planes to Chicago Midway and Champaign airports. United you'll be number one to land. Clear to start descent to three thousand, new runway is 32 left, surface winds seventy-five degrees at sixteen miles per hour, turn right to 140 degrees, level off at five for one minute, then turn right to 220 degrees. Level off at three thousand. This would put you on right base leg. Call when reaching three. Over."

"Thank you, approach, will see you in a bit. United 856."

The crew was ten miles out on the final approach as they prepared to land at O'Hare. The last half hour had been most frustrating for all aircraft who were holding for entrance into Chicago. Flying blind in a snowstorm is perhaps the most dreadful position any pilot, young or old, could be placed in. These skilled and brave pilots are trained every six months by their companies to perform in such situations. They are drilled constantly on precision flying, on taking control of situations regardless of the circumstances. But of course, training in a simulator is not the same as flying a real plane, and pilots, no matter what their training, intelligence, and skill, are mortal and fallible beings. Land was starting to take shape as visibility was clearing through patches of holes left by the clouds. Aligning the plane along its flight path, the crew by now needing a well-deserved breakfast was finally able to breathe a sigh of relief.

"Chicago approach control, 856 United leveling at three thousand heading 220 degrees, number one to land. Awaiting landing instruction, over."

"Roger, 856 United, approach has you on radar. Turn to frequency 118.1 for tower. Thank you for your patience and understanding, over."

"Thank you, approach, for your fine work. United turning to frequency 118.1. Good day."

"Chicago tower control, United flight 856 is with you on 118.1 number one to land. over."

"Roger, United 856, tower control, turn right 320 degrees for final into O'Hare, winds 227 degrees at twenty miles per hour, ILS to runway 32 left is active. Clear for outer-marker, over."

Roger, O'Hare, United 856 turning right to 320 degrees for final to ILS 32 left ADF, VOR, and outer-marker set.

The DC-8 was on its final approach: its landing gear was down, flaps and front slats were set. However, the runway was not in sight. If United 856 did not have visual, they would have to do a go-around, or possibly be diverted to another airport. That didn't look good to the crew, who had passengers and additional crew members waiting for the 9:00 a.m. to New York. Captain Sawyer looked at his two men and said, "Gentlemen, we need to land this plane in our first attempt, so I need a sharp eye for runway. Richard, I need you up here for backup."

For most pilots, a missed approach means a go-around, and a go-around in severe weather is disliked, to say the least. Tension mounts in the cockpit when a pilot, for any given reason, has to perform a go-around. Moreover, DC-8 did not respond well to that maneuver. To understand the difficulties and risk involved, one must imagine a plane on its final approach. The speed has been reduced to slow flight critical to flight, the flaps are extended downward, and the gears are in down position. This creates what is called slow drag, bringing the plane to the lowest rate of speed while still being able to maintain flight, enabling the crew to land without running out of runway. Now, imagine that you have to do a go-around. You have to clean the airplane add full throttle (power) while bringing the flaps and gears up as you navigate your way in thick clouds mixed with wind and rain. This must be done precisely or the aircraft can stall. The crew of United 856 did not want to face a go-around, nor did they want to run the risk of being diverted to another airport. They had to land. Suddenly the first officer, with a smile on his face and relief in his voice, said, "Skipper, runway in sight at eleven o'clock."

St. Joseph's Priory
Somerset, Ohio
Friday, December 16
6:51 a.m.

The trees at St. Joseph's Priory were frosted with snow, making the campus look like a picture-perfect postcard. The snow that had settled during the night was unmarred as the taxi arrived. Cab drivers who knew the place made certain they were on time regardless of weather, most likely because of a story told by a local cabbie. He claimed that a cab driver by the name of Jim was sent to pick up a priest from the St. Joseph's on Good Friday and take him to the airport. The priest was going home to spend Easter Sunday with friends and family members he had not seen in years. Apparently, Jim made an unscheduled stop at the corner bar before heading out to pick up the priest. Jim lost track of time at the pub, leaving the priest waiting, bags in hand, and ultimately causing the priest to miss his flight. Wondering what had happened, the priest called the cab company. Bewildered, the dispatcher radioed Jim. Two hours later, he was found asleep in his cab, drunk. He was fired on the spot, but the damage had been done. The priest had missed his flight and would not see his family that year.

Still intoxicated, Jim got into his own car, which was parked in the cab company's parking lot, and drove away. The next day his car was found with its wheels facing the sky. Inside lay Jim, his body badly bruised, his head covered with blood; he had hit a tree and rolled over. As he was being taken to the waiting ambulance, he mumbled to the officer taking his statement that a white dove had crashed into his car windshield, causing him to lose control. He died of his injuries on Easter Sunday. Investigators from the police department went back to the scene of the crash but found no dove. His case was ruled driving under the influence of alcohol.

Knocking on the door, the cab driver was anxious to get going. He knew that traffic was going to be rough going to the airport. Vincent called out the window that he'd be right down. Looking at his room for the last time, he grabbed his luggage and headed to Father Fitzgerald's quarters. Standing there a moment, he felt a sense of sadness; the priory and its members had been his family for the past six months. Hearing the driver honking the horn outside, Vincent broke from his reverie and knocked on the door. Father Fitzgerald opened the door, the look on his face showing he was expecting Vincent. Seeing Vincent's sad face, Father Fitzgerald gave him a strong hug and reassured him that everything was going to be all right.

Now listen, Vincent, the priest said, "I don't want you to leave with a guilty conscience. You have a long and healthy life ahead of you." He smiled and said, "Here is my number in case you need to talk. Don't forget us, okay?"

Vincent promised that he would not, and he kneeled in front of his mentor and kissed the priest's ring as a sign of love and respect. His friend and traveling companion, John, called from outside. Vincent grabbed his luggage and headed out the door. He was greeted with a snowball from John as the driver yelled for them to hurry up or they'd miss their flight. As the cab started to drive away, they could hear from the open window friends shouting good-bye. Some came out and started throwing snowballs at the cab as it drove away. Looking out from the back window they could see the campus getting smaller. There was no turning back now, and John and Vincent were quiet as they viewed the scenery, anxious to get to the airport and to begin their new life.

Jacob Riis Apartments
Lower East Side, Manhattan
Friday, December 16
6:55 a.m.

From the hallway window on the twelveth floor, where my father and I were waiting for the elevator, we could see the Williamsburg Bridge, aglow with headlights as cars crossed into Brooklyn. The compound in Jacob Riis was isolated, not a soul in sight, and I could tell that no one had left their apartments yet because there were no footprints in the snow. As we headed toward Avenue D and Seventh Street, I could see early-morning workers standing on the sidewalk, waiting for the city bus. I wondered how they could stand the cold.

Rosie's, the local candy store, was open and commuters walked in to buy newspapers or cigarettes. Located on Seventh Street and Avenue D, Rosie was well known for her delicious egg creams and fresh cookies. I don't know how long her shop had been there, but she was one smart lady, very business oriented. Daylight arrived as we arrived at the little store we owned. Dad had made lots of friends who, like most of us, worked for minimum wages. He understood their needs and catered to them, at times extending credit to them on a weekly basis. Winter was perhaps the hardest time for us because the excessive wind and cold as on this day would cause the locks and gates that protected the store to freeze up, so we would have to start the day trying to get them to unlock. And today the wind from the storm had also buried the entrance in snow.

While shoveling the snow from the entrance and clearing a path to the street, I could see stores opening for their daily business. Across the street was Molly's Restaurant, famous for Jewish food. On the corner of Seventh

Street was Harry's Delicatessen; they had the best kosher sandwiches. Ratners delicatessen, located on Delancey Street, was certainly the best on the Lower East Side, but Harry's was a close second. Everyone was busy shoveling snow from their sidewalk. Once inside the store, my job was to fill the refrigerator with the milk delivered early every morning. It was left in front of the store in ten plastic crates, each crate holding twenty containers of milk. Sometimes, I had to go to the basement which I never liked, because it reminded me of my old Dungeon to get supplies when we had to restock the shelves. When I was finished, I would go to school. But today I had no plans to attend school that day. The only thing that I was going to miss was the Christmas party and a chance to dance with Gloria, my girlfriend. After packing the milk into the refrigerator, I told my father that I was leaving, and extended my hand. He looked at me and handed me a dollar. As I was leaving, he reminded me that later that day I would be helping to stock cans of goods on the store shelves a truck was going to drop off our order for the month, approximately one hundred boxes. My job was to open every box, price every can, and stock them with their labels facing front and prices visible, and after that I had to dispose of the corrugated boxes. I hated that task. With a grimace, and a sense of guilt, I headed out of the store.

I headed toward Delancey Street to catch the BMT subway. With Christmas just around the corner, stores were opening earlier than normal and merchants were setting up shops on the sidewalks. The smell of pine was in the air from the vendor who was unloading trees and setting them to rest on the side of an abandoned building on Essex Street. The two most popular streets for shopping during the holiday season were Essex and Orchard Streets. Orchard Street was mainly dominated by Jewish vendors it is said that these merchants believed that for them to have a profitable day, they must always secure the first sale of the day, even if it meant losing a profit from its original price. Many shoppers, including my father, knew this and would take advantage of it as each tried to be the first in the store that morning. It was like competing for first prize. The streets were slushy from the snow and rain that had come down the night before. The streets looked gloomy, perhaps a sign of more snow.

Approaching Delancey, I had a feeling of apprehension mixed with guilt. I had never lied to my parents before. They gave me all the freedom that a fifteen-year-old was entitled to. My father trusted me, so the thought of facing him if I got caught made me tremble inside. With two dollars in my pockets, I headed down to the train station. I felt uncomfortable heading down into the dark station another Dungeon reminder but I purchased my token and continued to the train platform. The morning crowd was overwhelming as commuters prepared for another day at the office. As the train approached the platform, my nerves were at the edge. This was my first time traveling underground alone; my father prohibited me from traveling alone, saying I was too young. I could hear the train from a distance, its whistle getting louder and louder. Suddenly a tiny light appeared from the darkened tunnel. The train roared in with a tremendous sound, and you could feel the breeze hit your face from the speed the train carried. With traveling instructions given to me by Joaquin, I boarded the train. The doors slowly closed behind me, and as the train started to pull away from the station, a pleasant sensation came over me as I saw Delancey Street disappear from view. Finally I was heading toward Brooklyn, to shop for my bike. Everything was going according to plan. Now all I had to do was to wait for the conductor to say, Flatbush Ave.

I settled in a corner of the train as it roared toward Brooklyn. As I looked around, I could see the passengers all busy doing their own thing. Some were reading the morning newspaper while others kept to themselves. One passenger had a transistor radio, and I'll never forget the song that was playing on his AM radio that morning. It was the Shirelles singing their #1 hit, "Will You Still Love Me Tomorrow?" Inside the train, some anxiety was starting to settle in, as I now was convinced that there was no turning back. The hardest part was persuading myself that I could do this. This was an adventure to me, nothing more. As I looked around, feeling good about myself and what I had accomplished, a loud voice came through the speakers. It was the conductor, his voice blasting the interior of the train. "Flatbush Avenue next, Flatbush Avenue."

As I disembarked the train, I kept thinking about how good this day was going to be. All I had to do was find the bike shop, check the prices, and get back to Manhattan before noon. School was closing early that day because of the holiday, and my parents would be expecting me.

Paul Geidel
Sleight Avenue, Staten Island, NY
Friday, December 16
6:59 a.m.

Paul Geidel, a firefighter, stood composed at his kitchen window, surrounded by the silence and darkness of the early morning. He watched the snow as he drank a cup of black coffee and waited for his friend and coworker, Joe Reres, to pick him up. Paul had been up since 5:00 a.m., his home chores including feeding his eight-month-old daughter, Christine. His two sons, Ralph and Gary, were still sound asleep. Thinking of them, he reminisced about his teen years growing up in Staten Island, one of the five boroughs of New York. Born and raised in Staten Island, Paul was getting ready to commence his day shift with Rescue Company One in Manhattan. His thoughts were interrupted as he felt cold hands on his neck. Startled, he turned. It was his high school sweetheart and wife, Patricia, who had snuck into the kitchen and put her cold hands on the back of his neck. They had met at Tottenville High, where Paul pitched for the school softball team. They graduated in 1952 and began dating each other. In 1956 they married and settled into their new home on Sleight Avenue. That year luck struck the Geidels twice: Paul's lifelong dream came true he had been hired by the New York Fire Department and they were expecting their first child. Patricia reminded Paul that the driveway to their home needed to be shoveled before he left. He put down his cup of coffee, grabbed his winter coat, and headed out toward the door with shovel in hand. Rescue Company One was located in the heart of Manhattan and covered the entire eastern portion of it. While shoveling the snow, with his wife watching from the kitchen window, Paul's only thought was getting to his job. He had been drafted by his lieutenant,

Bill McMahon, to decorate the firehouse Christmas tree. Every year the men of Rescue One decorated the firehouse with presents and a ten-foot Christmas tree. The tree and presents were donations given by the locals and were to be handed out on Christmas Eve to less fortunate families. Looking up at the sky, Paul took a deep breath, enjoying the cold air that was coming from the north. The skies were deep purple as the light of daybreak tried to make its presence known. Paul noticed one of Gary's toys, a small replica of a fire truck, covered with snow. His two boys loved playing firemen, and they each had their very own plastic fire hats. Every night when he got home they would be wearing their hats, ready to play fireman with their hero dad. Gary, who was the oldest of the boys, was the most observant and imitated his father's every move; he also declared early on that he wanted to be a firefighter too, which pleased Paul but worried Patricia, who wanted them to be anything but firemen. The job was nerve-wracking for her, and, at times, lonely. She knew her husband's profession was an honorable one, but it was still hard and having one in the family was enough.

The morning was still dark when it was interrupted by the sound of tires crushing the snow on Sleight Avenue. It was Joe, his horn blasting as he approached his colleague's home. No matter how many times Paul told Joe not to blow his horn, Joe still did it, annoying Paul and the neighbors, who complained about the racket. Pulling up to the driveway Joe was met with a barrel of snowballs, Paul's way of retaliating for the noise. Leaving his truck running, Joe scrambled to safety as he rolled up some snowballs to counter Paul's attack. In no time the two were at each other as Patricia, laughing, looked on. By then the next door neighbor's German Shepherd began barking furiously; seeing this, the two firemen pummeled the dog with snowballs. Paul left his friend with the dog as he went inside to kiss his wife good-bye, stealing a sip of her coffee.

"Paul, don't forget to call the kids when you get to the station house, okay."

"Sure, honey. Today should be calm because I play elf for the lieutenant, remember? I have been drafted for community service. I should be home on schedule."

The horn sounded, a snowball hitting the vinyl siding of the house. Joe shouted, "Paul, we're going to be late, let's get going!"

Waving good-bye the two drove off, leaving Patricia and the rest of the neighbors to contend with the barking dog.

New York City Fire Department Background

In the early 1960s, there were more than one hundred thousand fires in America and one out of ten occurred in New York City. The men and women who fight these fires are the heart and soul of New York. They put their lives on the line every day as they combat the enemy they call The Red Devil. Driven by passion and dedication and withstanding pain and frustration beyond measure, they live to save lives, and the nobility of their occupation stimulates them to deeds of daring, even if it means the ultimate sacrifice.

Every day in New York, a battlefront is drawn somewhere, as buildings, some old and decrepit, some overcrowded, some abandoned, collapse from fires created by man. The battles are long and furious. The personal risks to the firefighters are enormous and at times costly. It's common for firefighters to arrive for a small fire and within moments, see it turn into a blazing inferno. Many of these fires are caused by careless people or arsonists out to destroy property. Vacant buildings are usually occupied by the homeless. They are also the drug dens of the addicted. But no matter what the circumstances, firemen rush to confront the raging beast, which spares no one. Whether fighting a fire in the high-rise building in Manhattan, a home in Bronx, or a brownstone in Brooklyn, these warriors never complain about its part of their job, a job they do with pride, strength, and courage.

In 1915, a special unit was assembled to combat situations of catastrophic magnitude. Applicants chosen for this job were of highest excellence. They were trained on how fire behaves. They studied building structures, bridges, water pipes; plumbing, and electricity, skills that were needed to close off pipes or remove broken wires. These men were prepared mentally to face the most horrendous situations imaginable. When the occasion arose, these were the men that would respond to the call disaster, the worst of events. At the scene itself, rescue companies prepare for search-and-rescue or search-and-recovery. They confront the forces in front of them, paving the way to search for survivors regardless of risk or outcome. As one firefighter put it,

"You can't negotiate with fire." We cannot imagine the horror of being surrounded by bodies, some burned beyond recognition, and parts of human flesh scattered within reach. To survive, these rescue workers must keep their emotions in check and rely on each other not only to get the job done but to survive. Their trust in each other is supreme, an essential ingredient, since no one, no matter how well trained, can be fully prepared for catastrophic events. They truly are the heroes of modern time.

Joseph Colacano
A Tree Farm
New Jersey
Friday, December 16
7:01 a.m.

The smell of pine made it evident that Christmas was approaching. The morning sun was rising from the east but the wind kept the air bitter. Snow from the previous night had left another white blanket wrapping the pine trees with its flakes, a picture-perfect setting. The small panel truck could hold only about ten more trees, and Joseph was finishing tying the backdoors together with rope to secure the trunks of the trees that were sticking out. John, in the tree farm's office, was paying the owner for the fifty trees that he and Joseph had just purchased. This was the first time both men had visited a tree farm, and as they stood there in the middle of it, looking into the cold gray sky, the two men could hear the sound of birds interrupting the silence around them. Looking at John, Joseph said, "You know, John, I could stay here forever."

"Yeah, me too, but not today. Let's get some coffee before we head back to Brooklyn."

Getting out of the farm was tricky; it was like a maze. There were only three things you could see—the sky, the ground, and the trees—and not knowing the route would mean time lost. The farm had two roads leading in and out, and John was taking extra time driving on the dirt road, which was covered with snow and rain, making it hard to drive on. Driving on this type of road had John worried; he didn't want to get stuck in the mud. The road seemed long and narrow as the two boys inched closer to the exit of the maze.

The trip back to New York in these conditions would take approximately two hours. The cousins had been on the road since 5:30 a.m.; both had been up since 4:00 a.m. This was going to be a long and cold day, but their goal was to sell the trees and make the profit. Approaching the turnpike John noticed a sign reading Chock Full of Nuts, turn right. Both men were cold and hungry, so Joseph turned off the main road and into the Chock Full of Nuts driveway, and gave John money to buy coffee and donuts.

"Make it to go, John," said Joseph. "We only have two hours to set up business in Brooklyn."

Coffee and donuts in hand and only twenty dollars left in his pocket, Joseph headed toward Brooklyn with John to set up shop and begin selling their trees. Taking the New Jersey Turnpike, the two excited and anxious to get to Brooklyn. The morning was getting warmer as the two approached Newark. Looking to his left, John could see Newark International Airport and he commented on how quiet it looked. He thought it was perhaps shutdown because of weather, but to his amazement, he noticed an Eastern Airline DC-8 taking off. Tapping his uncle on the shoulder, John pointed to the jet taking off. Joseph slowed down to see the beauty of the big white-and-blue plane's takeoff, and they watched with interest until the plane vanished into the clouds, the sound of its turbines still audible. They drove on, following the sign that read: Holland Tunnel to New York.

Steven Baltz
Wilmette, Illinois
Friday, December 16
7:11 a.m.

With the luggage placed beside the door, Steven Baltz was upstairs, tying his shoes. Unable to sleep the night before and hyper in the morning, Steven had been up at the break of day. His father, William, was already in the kitchen having coffee that Pearl Belue, the maid, had brewed. All through the night the howling wind had made it impossible for William Sr. to sleep. The side streets were covered with snow and rain, and the only visible traffic was the sanitation crew cleaning the streets. You could hear the wind brushing across the trees near the house. Inside Pearl hurried to prepare breakfast for the two boys and their father. The aroma of coffee blended with bacon wafted through the house, along with the noise of crackling eggs on the frying pan and the toast in the toaster. The trip to the airport was about an hour away, but the weather was playing a big factor in the morning rush. The snow had let up during the night, but news of more snow was heard over the kitchen radio. The one-hour drive was of little concern to William Baltz; his concern was for his son, who was flying alone for the first time. In their room, Steven's younger brother, William Jr., was combing his hair as he prepared to go to school. This was his last day before the holiday recess. Pearl was nervously giving instructions to little Steven, telling him to listen to the flight attendant and to wait in one place for his mother. Steven's father, worried, told Pearl to make sure to be at William's school in time to pick him up.

"Don't worry, Mr. Baltz," said Pearl. "You take Steven to the airport before he misses his flight."

Steven called out to his brother, who was still upstairs getting his coat; he wanted to say good-bye. William ran down the stairs with a watch belonging to Steven in his hand.

"Hey Stevie, you forgot your watch."

"Thanks, Billy, I almost forgot it."

From the kitchen, Pearl interrupted the boy's conversation. "Billy, come get your breakfast, or you'll be late for school. And let your brother go. He'll miss his plane."

Billy's reply astounded Pearl and his father, who was at the door with luggage in hand. "I hope he does. I don't want him to go, Aunt Pearl."

Pearl, stunned by his remarks, approached Billy and, kneeling down, looked at the young boy who had tears in his eyes and said, "Billy, why would you say something like that?"

"I don't want him to go. I'm scared something will happen to him."

Standing by the door, Steven looked confused, not knowing why his brother would say those words. His father, on hearing his son's plea for his brother to stay home and go to school with him, set Steven's luggage aside and approached his youngest son.

Placing his hand on his son's shoulder, William looked at him and said, "Son, your brother will be all right. Besides, he's only gonna be gone for a week. Before you know it he'll be back, okay?"

Still looking teary, Billy said, "But Dad, what if something happens?"

"Nothing is going to happen, Billy."

As the two headed out the door, Steven ran back in and up the stairs to his room to the dresser where his piggy bank stood, and took out his savings, sixty-five cents. He put the change in his pocket and ran out of the house to meet his dad for the trip to the airport.

Darnell Mallory
University of Omaha
Omaha, Nebraska
December 16
7:16 a.m.

The musical instruments lay on the stage, the red, white, and blue balloons still clinging to the ceiling, and graffiti scattered around the dance floor. The celebration had continued through the night as the students danced the night away. The lack of sleep wasn't a concern for most, as they would be traveling to their holiday destinations by bus or train, giving them a chance to sleep on the way.

His heart beating with anxiety, Darnell waited for his cab to arrive. He had called them early, fearing that the weather would delay his trip to Chicago's airport. He was excited to be going home. Looking out the window, he could see birds nesting on top of a tree facing his room, their wings mantling to keep from being blown off their home. The wind was shifting the tree back and forth, a sign that it was cold outside. A knock on the door broke his concentration. It was Tom, who was splitting the cab fare to the airport with him. With coffee and donuts in hand for himself and his traveling friend Darnell, bought from the cafeteria, Tom expressed some concern for the weather. Looking out the window side by side, the young freshmen gathered their thoughts while drinking their coffee. In the hallway outside the room, they could hear the commotion as students hustled to get to their destinations on time. A knock on the door eased the tension; it was Judy, one of the cheerleaders who was leaving for California to be with her family. With bags in tow, Judy ran over to Darnell, wishing him and Tom a safe trip. Opening the door, she ran out just as fast as she had run in, disappearing into the crowd. The two were left alone again, waiting for their cab to show up.

Tom broke the silence by asking Darnell a personal question. "So, Darnell, am I to assume that you're going to hanky panky this holiday?"

Darnell, embarrassed by Tom's question, replied, with a half smile, "I guess you'll have to wait till I get back for the answer, Tommy boy." "Anyway," Darnell continued, "Shirley Dean and I plan to get engaged. That's the right way for a man to treat the woman of his dreams. I'm going to propose to her on Christmas Eve."

With that the two shook hands, Tom being the first to congratulate him.

"Now hold on, Tom. Congratulate me when I get back. She hasn't said yes yet."

"I know, buddy," said Tom. "But just in case I don't see you again, you know."

Surprised, Darnell replied, "What are you talking about, idiot? You aren't planning to not come back."

"Of course, I'm coming back, idiot, but it's just that I get scared to fly, especially in this type of weather."

"Listen, Tom, you and I will be perfectly safe on those planes. They're equipped with good pilots and they're new, remember? They're brand new; what could possibly happen?"

Their conversation came to a sudden halt as a loud horn echoed inside the dorm. It was their cab, waiting outside.

Port Columbus Airport
Departure Terminal, Gate 9
December 16
8:14 a.m.

The terminal was buzzing as passengers waited for their flights to be announced. The weather outside the terminal was gray and cold as snow mixed with hail and heavy clouds were visible. Everyone around was smiling, Christmas spirit in the air. A crowd had gathered around Gate 9, which was one of the first flights to leave. TWA 266, due to depart at 9:00 a.m., was still being loaded with luggage and food to be served during the morning run. The crew was already aboard, preparing to greet the passengers heading to New York. On the deck were Captain Wollam, First Officer Bowen, and Flight Engineer Leroy Rosenthal. Patricia Post, along with Margaret Gernat, was making last-minute adjustments in the cabin. The crew had arrived from Dayton just a few hours ago, but was ready to go into New York, their home base and residence. Pat was going to spend the holidays in her cozy apartment at Seventy-sixth Street and Jackson Heights in Queens, while Margaret was going to her parents' house in Granville, New York. Back in the terminal, the crowd was getting bigger by the minute, as the time of departure approached. Silence fell through the terminal as all ears focused on the female voice, coming over the loudspeaker.

Good morning, ladies and gentleman, Port Columbus Airport happily announces the departures of TWA Flight 266 for LaGuardia Airport in New York, now boarding Gate 9, and Pan-Am Flight 811 for Duluth, Minnesota, boarding Gate 12.

Applause broke out at the announcement and passengers and well wishers began to embrace each another, wishing each other happy holidays.

Vincent Flood gave his friend John a hug as they got ready to board their separate planes.

"Make sure you call me when you get home, okay, Vincent?"

Vincent replied by shaking John's hand and saying, "John, promise me that you'll keep in touch, and yes, I'll call you."

A line was starting to form as they went their separate ways. At the courtesy counter of TWA, Arthur Swenson was checking in. Traffic had been horrendous; snow and sleet had kept him from getting to the airport an hour before departure as was customary with the airlines.

Flight 266 was due to depart Port Columbus Airport at 0900 hours, with thirty-nine passengers aboard. The gross weight for takeoff was 101,444 pounds, including twenty-six hundred pounds in fuel for the one-hour-and-thirty-two-minute trip. Captain Wollam and his crew were advised by flight control that this was going to be a flight under instrument flight rules and that their altitude would be seven thousand feet. Their clearance was to via Appleton, Ohio, Vector 12 to Johnstown, Vector 106 by way of Selinsgrove into Vector 6 Pennsylvania, and finally Vector 123 to LaGuardia Airport. The crew was awaiting instruction from Port Columbus departure control to start the engines. Back in the cabin, Patricia and Margaret were securing items for takeoff, only minutes away. They also distributed blankets so passengers would stay warm during the flight. Cabin heat was just starting to come on. When Patricia stopped to give a couple a blanket for their infant, she picked him up from his mother's lap and asked her the baby's name.

"Tracy Lee Mullins," the young mother replied. The couple was making a stopover in New York, where they were connecting to a flight to Puerto Rico; they were visiting her parents, who had never seen the newborn.

Everyone on board was happy that they were finally getting underway. Looking out the window, the captain could see patches of clouds starting to close in, and he was worried that they might be grounded due to weather. He called Margaret onto the deck and asked how the passengers were.

"They're all excited and anxious to get on their way," she replied with a big smile.

"Don't get your hopes up high," said Dave Wollam. If we don't get started within the next two minutes, we might be here awhile.

"TWA 266, Port Columbus, you're clear to start engines?"

Dean Bowen replied, "Roger, Columbus, TWA 266 clear to start engines."

Back at the gate, a crowd of well wishers waved as the engines came to life, a visible puff of white smoke spurting from the engines.

"TWA 266, Columbus ground control, clear to taxi, runway five, winds 120 degrees at 20 miles per hour, and altimeter is 31.09. You'll be number one for takeoff. Contact departure at 123.8. Good day."

O'Hare Airport
Chicago, Illinois
December 16
8:27 a.m.

The fifty-foot tower stood alone, the wind rattling the glass windows as the snow clobbered the tall thin building from all sides. On this gloomy morning, air traffic controllers were busy with binoculars in one hand and mikes in the other as they directed traffic en route. Despite all the noise inside the glassy tower, Bob Fiebling had isolated himself with his thoughts. Viewing the scene from inside the warm tower, the first officer drank a warm cup of coffee and stared at the closed runway, where a Pan Am jet had skidded earlier. He watched as the ground crew slowly towed the crippled jet to safety, then switched his focus to the blue-and-white DC-8 below. It was his flight, 826. Bob checked his watch and noted that he had less than thirty minutes before takeoff.

Looking up at the sky, he noticed that the winds had let up a bit and the snow was coming down more gently. He was still feeling a little hyper from their arrival in Chicago the last fifteen minutes of the flight had been brutal, although the crew had seen worse. He admired the jet below. "How beautiful she looks," he thought, "and how well she handles." From the side door leading to the ramp, he spotted his captain, Robert Sawyer, approaching the plane to start the pre-flight inspection. As he watched the captain, he thought: "Poor chap, he forgot his coat." The captain had no umbrella, either, and it was only about twenty degrees outside.

His attention was pulled back to the tower with the voice of John, one of the meteorologists stationed at O'Hare. Startled, Bob spilled his coffee. John's expression said he had news for the crew and passengers. Finished with his pre-flight inspection, Captain Sawyer and his second officer, Richard Prewitt, were having coffee in the pilots lounge and listening to the weather over the airport waveband. The crew's first leg into Chicago was a bit rough, and the trip to New York was to be less so. The winds had died down and visibility was moderate. A blast of dry and puffy snow along the East Coast was expected, however. The captain had instructed Prewitt to file a report about the VOR that had malfunctioned en route. Prewitt had already filled out the report and had suggested as well that a complete inspection of the exterior of the plane be made upon their arrival at Idlewild, which the captain confirmed with a nudge of his hat. A knock on the plate glass to the lounge got their attention; it was Mary Mahoney and the other stewardesses, Augustine Ferrer, Anne Bouthen, and Patricia Keller. They were heading to the plane, which now had converted to United 826; they were met by Bob, who had just exited the tower. He motioned the captain and the second officer to join the crowd, pointing to his watch. Meanwhile, in the passengers' lounge, in a corner next to a United attendant, William Baltz was kneeling down, giving his son Steven final instructions before the attendant walked him onto the plane and turned him over to the stewardesses.

"Make sure you stay with one of the stewardesses until Mommy comes, okay?"

"Okay, Dad."

Bill rose to his feet as the attendant took Steven by hand and led him to the plane. Bill felt a lump in his throat when his son turned to wave to him as he was being led onto the DC-8. His view was suddenly obstructed by a tall young man running, carrying luggage, toward the check-in lane; it was Darnell Mallory. His cab had been caught in a traffic accident, and for a moment it had seemed like Darnell and his friend Tom would have to run the rest of the way to the airport. Coming to a stop in front of the baggage check-in, Darnell waved to Tom, who was also running toward his line.

"Hey Tom!" Darnell shouted. "See you in two!"

Looking down at the entrance to the plane, Darnell saw Steven being led in. Steven looked at Darnell and smiled; Darnell, returning the courtesy, gave him a wink.

"Good morning, ladies and gentleman. United 826, departing at nine eleven to Idlewild New York, now boarding Gate 9."

Brookfield Road
Glastonbury, CT.
December 16
8:51 a.m.

The streets leading to Brookfield Road were still cluttered with snow from the previous night and the wind twisted the Christmas ornaments from their foundations with a vengeance, tossing the remaining snowflakes into the air, making it difficult to walk and drive. The cars were covered with snow, their owners deciding this was a good reason to have a long weekend. Parking her car in the driveway, Virginia headed toward the entrance to the family house. Leaving her galoshes neatly alongside the porch, she headed immediately to the kitchen for a cup of tea. She had just finished dropping off the children at school, and was now taking time to relax before heading out again to the grocer. Looking at the kitchen clock, which read 8:51 a.m., Virginia's mind went to her husband's whereabouts, wondering if Arthur had made it to the airport in time. Her plans to drive to New York to pick him up were demolished by his decision for her not to make the 100-mile trip in bad weather. Moving to the living room, Virginia turned on the television, tuning to news of the weather. Leaning over to adjust the volume to the tube, she wondered what impact the weather would have on her husband's flight. The news announced that a storm was possible for the East Coast. Outside the window, a sanitation truck went by with its wide shovel, removing the snow from the road and scattering salt in its wake. Today, she thought to herself, I think I'll make a special dinner for my family. Putting her coat on, Virginia leaned over, turned off the television, and headed out into the cold.

Port Columbus Airport
TWA 266
December 16
9:01 a.m.

The roar of the four engines penetrated the interior of the Lockheed Constellation, its massive Wright engines slowly taxiing the massive aircraft to its active runway. The Super Constellation had been stationed on the tarmac since it had landed at 6:00 a.m. from Dayton, Ohio. The plane had been deiced twice. Maintenance crews had to remove the snow that had accumulated on top of the wings. Earlier the plane had been pumped with twenty-six hundred pounds of fuel, and luggage loaded into its compartment. The distance to the active runway seemed far, a thin layer of lights partially obscured by the grayish snow that had been stacked alongside the runway by ground crews. Inside the cabin all eyes were on Margaret Gernat, one of the stewardesses, as she gave the final instructions to her passengers before takeoff. Her co-worker and friend Patricia Post was busy checking for loose items, making sure everything was secured. Midway down the cabin, seated by a window, lost in his thoughts, Vincent Flood was observing the view, his mind wandering away from Margaret's introduction to flight safety. Enjoying the view from his seat, Vincent was examining the length of the right wing, which carried two of the prop engines, the wing bouncing up and down slightly as the plane hit potholes leading to the active runway. Vincent noticed a Pan-Am jet starting its takeoff roll, its nose rotating toward the gray sky. With a smile he mumbled to himself, "Safe trip, buddy."

He was referring to his friend John, who was headed home aboard the Pan-Am that had just disappeared into the dingy morning clouds and out of view. Seated across him was Arthur Swenson. He too was sitting privately with his thoughts, also observing the outside view. His mind was on his home in Connecticut and how desperately he wanted to be back home with his wife and three children. His reverie was interrupted by the sound of a child crying.

The mother was holding her daughter on her lap, while her husband, seated by the window, was trying to reach the child's pacifier, which had dropped to the middle of the aisle. Reaching for the pacifier, Arthur got off his seat and handed it to the mother. With a kind smile she thanked him. Arthur asked, "How old is your daughter?"

"She's almost two weeks," she replied.

"My name is Arthur Swenson. You have a lovely daughter."

"Thank you. My name is Karen Grieble, this is my husband Peter; and this is Christine."

Just then Margaret touched Arthur on the shoulder, letting him know it was time to return to his seat and buckle up. The cabin was buzzing with excitement as the passengers carried on many conversations at once, making it difficult to distinguish a clear sentence among all the words. Meanwhile, up front on the flight deck, the crew was busy preparing the plane for takeoff. It was customary on each flight for the captain to come on the intercom with a few words for the passengers. Approaching the runway ramp, the captain gave control to his first officer while he took the mike to introduce himself.

"Good morning, ladies and gentleman, this is your captain speaking. My name is David Wollam, and on behalf of the crew and myself, I want to take this opportunity to welcome you aboard TWA Flight 266 inbound to LaGuardia Airport in New York. Our approximate time en-route is one hour and thirty minutes, we'll be flying at an altitude of seven thousand feet, and cruising comfortably at three hundred miles per hour. The weather in New York is much the same, snow mixed with rain, temperature twenty-nine degrees, the high reaching forty." Pause. "Ladies and gentleman, we have just been informed by tower controller that we are number one for takeoff, so sit back, relax, and enjoy the flight, thank you."

In the cabin, the passengers welcomed the news with thunderous applause. In the front of the cabin, Patricia was warming up a bottle of milk for one of the passengers who was traveling with her infant son. She was trying to close the cap to the bottle while maintaining her balance as the Connie plane slowly made its way to the active runway. Margaret motioned her to hurry. The FAA requires every person to be seated and strapped in during takeoff, including crew members. Walking down the aisle toward seat 29A, swinging side to side, Patty handed the bottle to Juanita Mullins, as her husband Cecil gave her a smile of gratitude. Giving the infant a soft pinch on the cheek, Patricia smiled and headed toward her station for takeoff.

"TWA 266, this is Port Columbus departure control, taxi to active and hold, over."

"Roger, Columbus, taxi and hold 266."

Making a ninety-degree turn, the mammoth plane rattled inside as its engines were revved up to compensate for the turn onto the active runway.

"Mr. Rosenthal," said the captain. "How are those engines doing, sir?"

"Well, skipper," said the second officer. "Everything from back here is a go."

Looking out the window to his left, the captain could see the terminal, with its planes waiting to be boarded, and thought how happy he was to be leaving it to go home to New York. Sitting at the captain's right was his first officer, Dean Bowen, who was busy calculating the time and speed it would take to arrive on schedule. His trip to Glen Cove, Long Island, where he lived, was going to be a difficult one since his wife Mary Ellen, who had been planning to pick him up, had to stay home instead with their two daughters, who had come down with the flu. For Patricia Post, the trip from the airport to her house in Jackson Heights was going to be a cinch, since bus lines from LaGuardia to Queens were operable. David, the captain, not feeling well and possibly coming down with the flu, had called his wife Nanette to pick him up. His seven-year-old son Richard reminded his father of his promise to him and his older sister Dana about meeting Santa, who was appearing at Macy's Fifth Avenue.

"TWA 266, Columbus tower, you're clear for takeoff, let us know when rolling, over."

With its nose pointed down the ten-thousand-foot runway, the captain asked his first officer for an additional ten degrees on the flaps as he throttled up, waking up the Connie's engines.

'Columbus departure, 266 is now rolling. Good day.'

408 Broad Street
Summit, New Jersey
The Mallory Residence
December 16
9:05 a.m.

All by herself in her home, Annie-Lou was making last-minute preparations for the arrival of her son Darnell, who was coming home from the University of Omaha in Nebraska. Her other son, William Jr., had arrived last night from Kansas, where he attended college. Her daughter had gone to work in New York, and her youngest child Johnny was a student at Summit High.

Looking out the window with concern, Annie picked up the phone to call her husband, who had left early to work at the Ford automotive assembly in Linden, New Jersey. She had wondered why he had even gone to work when they had to pick Darnell up at the airport at 10:30 a.m. She knew by looking at the street that the driving would be slow heading into New York's Idlewild Airport in Queens. Unable to hold her anxiety, she dialed the plant to speak to her husband, William Sr. To her surprise, the phone rang as she was about to pick up the receiver. It was her daughter Mordine calling from the school where she worked. She sounded surprised that her mother was still home.

"Mom, what are you still doing home?"

"I'm waiting for your father to arrive." Her mom's voice sounded a little annoyed. "I told him not to go to work, but he did anyway."

Mordine had called to tell her mother that traffic going into the city was a bit hectic. She also reminded her mother to tell her father to take it easy driving. The roads were slippery due to the freezing rain. Her mother assured her that they would take her advice, and told her daughter to do the same heading home. Just then William Jr. walked in the house, and was also surprised that his mother was still home. On seeing his mother's expression, William decided to walk right by her, leaving her with her anger aimed at his father. Halfway to his room his mother called out his name. "William," she said, "make sure you pick up your brother from school. I don't know what time your father and I will be getting back."

Removing his wool hat, William replied with a half grin, "Mom, Johnny's a big boy now. He doesn't need to be picked up."

Frustrated by her husband's delay, Annie shouted back, "Just pick him up, William."

William decided to change the topic. "Hey Mom, what did you do to this house? It looks great. And hey, what's for dinner tonight? I haven't had a good meal in weeks."

Flashing him a look of disappointment, Annie placed her hands on her hips and struck back. "Stop the bull, William, you had a good meal last night; it's Darnell that hasn't had a good meal, in months, not weeks."

Laughing at her remarks, William turned to go into his room. Just then William Sr. came through the door, expecting a tongue-lashing from his wife. Knowing this, William Jr. ducked into his room; he didn't want to be in his father's shoes. Not today.

O'Hare Airport
Chicago, Gate 8
December 16
9:07 a.m.

United 826 was starting to board, so passengers made the trip to the ramp toward the DC-8 parked at Gate 8. The tarmac leading to the plane was slippery from the rain that had frozen into ice on the walkway. On top of the aluminum stairs leading to the jet, senior stewardess Mary Mahoney, holding her hat with one hand against the vigorous wind, was greeting the passengers who were scrambling to get out of the cold weather hounding them. Inside Anne Bouthen and Patricia Keller were busy getting the cabin ready for the boarding passengers, many requesting blankets to keep warm. Down on the tarmac at the beginning of the stairs, Augustine Ferrar, another stewardess, was advising the passengers to slow down, warning them of the ice on the stairs leading to the cabin.

Trying to cover her eyes from the twisting wind mixed with snow swirling around her, Augie, as she was called, could see the dark clouds hovering over the airport, and was wondering if a cancellation was coming. Inside, Stephen Baltz had already secured his place in the plane. He had gotten special attention due to his age. He was also required to have a name tag around his collar, letting the crew know that he was a minor flying alone. Reaching the inside, passengers could view the entrance to the cockpit. The doors were still open and the crew was busy talking to controllers inside the tower as they prepared for their final leg into New York. The chief mechanic was inside the cockpit getting the signature and approval from the captain on the jet's fuel consumption. As the mechanic exited the plane, Mary approached the captain, advising him that all passengers were accounted for.

"How many passengers do we have today, Mary?"

"We have sevety-seven, sir, one minor, flying alone."

Turning his attention to Mary, the first officer asked, "How's the little guy doing?"

The captain interrupted, "Yeah, Mary, and whose turn is it to babysit?"

Mary replied, "Me."

Trying to maintain a poker face, Robert, with a gleaming smile, said, "Mary, you have no kids, right?"

Sensing that she was being led into a trap, Mary replied, "No, sir."

"Well, Mary," said the captain, "you have one today, at least for a couple of hours."

Unable to control himself, Richard Prewitt, the second officer, burst out laughing as Mary made a face, sticking her tongue out at them and crossing her eyes in retribution.

"Okay guys," the captain said, "play time is over. Let's head to New York."

"Hey Mary," he added, "we're only kidding. I'm sure you'll make a fine mom."

"Mary, you still haven't answered my question," said Fiebling.

"What question was that?" she replied.

"How's the little guy doing?"

"Actually, he's excited about the whole thing."

"Hey, Mom," said the captain, "when we're straight and level, bring him in here. We'd like to meet him."

Closing the door behind him, Richard, the flight engineer, took out his engineer's flight manual to the DC-8, giving him control of the four jet engines for the startup sequence. A slight thump alerted the crew and passengers that the plane was being pulled to a clear area, where they would taxi to the active runway. As the jetliner approached the apron ramp to the active runway, the crew of three put their hands together one on top of each other, their ritual as their flight was about to start.

"United 826, this is O'Hare departure control, you're clear for takeoff, advise when wheels are up, over."

"Roger, O'Hare, United 826, heavy here we go."

TWA 266
Vector 12
Johnstown, PA
Seven Thousand Feet
9:21 a.m.

TWA 266 departed Port Columbus Airport at 9:00 a.m., EST. The gross weight at takeoff was 101,444 pounds, including twenty-six hundred gallons of fuel. The aircraft was within weight and balance limitations in accordance with current procedures. Time en route to LaGuardia was estimated to be one hour and thirty-two minutes. The TWA flight plan specified Instrument Flight Rules (IFR) at seven thousand feet. The clearance was to the New York Airport via Appleton, Ohio; Vector 12 Johnstown, in Pennsylvania, proceeding to Vector 106 Selinsgrove, also in Pennsylvania, and finally Vector 123 into LaGuardia. Subsequently, the altitude to the New York area was changed due to winds to seventeen thousand feet.

"Altoona Flight Control, Trans-World Airline Flight 266 is with you at 118.1, inbound to LaGuardia New York, over."

The Super Constellation with its thirty-nine passengers and a crew of five had reached its cruising altitude, recommended by Ohio's meteorologist and Flight 266 co-pilot Dean Bowen, in accordance with the flight's distance. Trying to shut out the noise of the propellers hammering the inside, some passengers were privately dealing with their own thoughts while others' laughter could be heard across the aisle of the cabin. Conversations ranged from Christmas presents to a cozy bedroom with a bottle of wine and a good book. At the front of the cabin, Margaret and Patricia were getting ready to serve breakfast, made up of coffee, juice, and danish rolls. Although it was only 9:30 a.m., the morning had been a long one, for the crew had been up for six hours already, departing Dayton Ohio Airport at 4:45 a.m. for Columbus. Most of the passengers had also been up early for the flight to New York.

"TWA 266, Altoona flight control, roger, we have you on 118.1, turn heading zero-eight-zero, climb to 17,000, frequency 121.1 to Vector 106 Selinsgrove, Pennsylvania, over."

"Roger, Altoona, TWA 266, I thought we were set for seven thou, over."

"TWA, Altoona control, gentlemen, you're going to have to climb to recommended altitude, turbulence en route up to fifteen thousand, reported from traffic heading west, over."

"Roger, Altoona, TWA turning left to zero-eight-zero, leaving seven for 17,000, Vector 106 to Selinsgrove Station, thank you and good day."

Juanita Mullins, seated with a window view over the right wing, had adjusted herself to the sound of the two propeller-driven engines. Petrified of flying, Juanita, with her husband Cecil and their newborn son, were heading to New York to connect with another flight to Puerto Rico, where her parents lived. Her aunt in New York was going to make the trip to LaGuardia to see the couples newborn for the first time. Looking up at the gloomy sky, she noticed the morning sun trying to penetrate through the clouds. The sun, she noticed, was shaped in the form of a glittering cross, sent from heaven. Cuddling her three-month-old son, Juanita made the sign of the cross as her husband slept.

With its engines on full throttle, the captain navigated the Super Constellation to its assigned altitude. The crew and passengers felt the strain being produced by the plane as the winds tossed the plane from side to side. The cabin fell silent as passengers gripped the sides of their chairs with white knuckles as they climbed toward the sky, away from the earth. Seated three seats behind the Mullins, Arthur Swenson brushed off the unpleasant climb that had caused him to feel nauseous. Unable to deal with the sensation of nausea, Arthur raised his hand to get the attention of Patricia, who was seated at the front of the cabin. Unbuckling her seat belt, Patricia went over to her passenger, who by now was visibly pale.

"I need to go to the bathroom, miss."

Concerned, Patricia asked, "What's the problem, sir?"

Half embarrassed, Arthur replied, "I think I'm going to throw up, miss."

"I can't allow you to get up from your seat while we're climbing, sir, captain's orders. How about a baggy?"

"No," he politely replied, "how much longer do we have to climb before I can get up?"

"The captain will turn off the seatbelt sign," she said, pointing to the sign at the front of the aisle. Just then a bell sounded and the sign flashed on and off, indicating that movement in the cabin was allowed. With that, Arthur raced to the front restroom. The Constellation had reached its assigned altitude of seventeen thousand feet.

United 826
Ohio Air Space
December 16
9:47 a.m.

United 826 departed Chicago's O Hare Airport at 9:11 a.m. A cruising flight level of twenty-seven thousand feet was attained at 9:36 a.m. The flight to the New York area was normal for the crew, with the exception of the wind momentum that had hampered them coming into Chicago. The two hour flight to Idlewild was to begin with Instrument Flight Rules (IFR) and end the same. The actual takeoff weight on the DC-8 was 214,790 pounds, which included 63,700 pounds of fuel, 6,450 pounds of cargo, plus passengers and crew. The maximum allowable takeoff weight was computed as 217,200 pounds. United 826 was within weight and balance limitations in accordance with current procedures.

The weather heading into the New York area was reported as heavy with snow flurries mixing with condensed rain. The crew had elected to use jet altitudes, due to the gusting winds up to twenty thousand feet. The United flight plan was to follow an easterly heading of 090 degrees via Ohio space control into Vector 55 and jet route 60 in Pennsylvania, via Allentown Vector, direct to Robbinsville 123, to Preston Intersection, and finally to Idlewild approach control.

Leveling off to its altitude of twenty-seven thousand feet, the crew was adjusting its DC-8 for straight and level flight. They had now reached their assigned altitude and a speed of five hundred miles per hour. Up above was a crystal-clear blue sky and a streaking ray of sunlight. The engines were running smoothly, and the passengers and the crew of seven were enjoying the comfort of the jetliner. Within less than an hour, United 826 would be stationed on the ground at New York's Idlewild Airport. For Captain Sawyer and his two crew members, the day would come to an end in less than an hour. Staring out the left window as the plane cruised on auto-pilot, Robert glanced at the clouds below him and thought about how peaceful it was there. Everything was on schedule and the silence of the air and the sweet murmuring of the turbines soothed his mind, putting him at ease. The glare of the sun coming up in the east forced the pilots and the flight engineer to don their sunglasses. Richard Prewitt was leaving his station to piss, as he called it, when an alarmed first officer called out to him, "Hey, Dick, the VOR is acting up again!"

Leaning forward to take a better look at the console and the number two VOR, Richard didn't know what to make of it. The needle had gone dead. Removing his shades, the concerned captain leaned over to tap the glass plate that protected the VOR from outside particles, hoping that the tapping would jar the needle back to its center. Fearing the possibility that the needle could be permanently damaged, the captain instructed the second in command, Robert Fiebling, to get out navigational charts for Pennsylvania, New Jersey, and New York, saying, "Bobby, I'm going to give it thirty minutes; if Richard can't fix it, I want you to tell me at all times where we are, okay?"

Robert assured the captain a fix at all times. Looking at both men, the skipper assured his crew that this was a minor situation, one that they train for in simulators. Shifting his eyes to Richard, his trusted engineer, the skipper said, "Get your flashlight out and check for blown fuses. Check any burned or loose wires running to the instrument panel." Although they didn't know it, the crew of 826 problems were not minor, as expected. With gusting winds and blinding snow, United 826 was approaching critical times ahead.

Systems of United 826

The navigational and communication equipment of Flight 826 consisted of some typical DC-8 installations incorporating minor changes in accordance with United Airlines policy.

Navigational equipment consisted of Automatic Directional Finder (ADF); Very high frequency omnidirectional range receiver (VOR); Instrument Landing System (ILS); and a gyro-stabilized compass system. Two complete sets of these units form the navigation system and they are referred to as System No. 1 and System No. 2. Note: The DC-8 was also equipped with weather radar for storm-monitoring.

The crew in fact was now faced with two crucial problems: an inoperable VOR, critical to navigation en route, and blinding snow. Unaware of the situation, the flight attendants were getting ready to serve breakfast to their seventy-seven cold and hungry passengers.

Systems of TWA 266

Model L-1049A: The Connie, as it was called, made its maiden flight in October 1950. The panel consisted of over forty dials and switches, all vital to the performance of the Constellation. The cockpit or flight deck, as it was called, was a bit cramped for the crew, which consisted of three individuals. Although it was slow, cruising at only 366 miles per hour, the Super Constellation 1049A had a maximum range of five thousand miles nonstop. Its triple rudder fins made it stable and secure on wide turns, but in shifting winds the opposite occurred.

The four propellers mounted on its wings rattled the ears of anyone seated next to them. The console looked like that of a military aircraft, its switches and dials almost impossible to define. Pilots who were rated in this type of aircraft knew the dos and don'ts while maneuvering the Connie in flight. On the ground, it had its drawbacks, taxiing was one of them. Making short turns while maneuvering around the terminal was a problem. Visibility was also a big concern, because the view from the inside was cut off by the small windows. Pilots complained that on final approaches the view was lost due to the construction of the cockpit. With the jet era fast approaching, the old workhorse was being phased out of commercial flying. Its next task would be cargo flying, which it is still used for today. I recall flying in the Connie coming from Puerto Rico with my parents. The rattling sound was unbearable, but all in all it was one of the safest planes ever built.

Rescue Company One
Manhattan
43 West Thirty-third Street
December 16
9:51 a.m.

The morning commute was unpleasant, pedestrians trying in vain to protect their heads with their umbrellas or newspapers, which they normally purchased at the train station to read on their way to work. Their scarves were wrapped around their mouths and they walked gingerly on the slippery sidewalks, while merchants, shovels in hand, were pushing the wet snow into the gutter, providing a cleaner and safer walkway for their customers. The Thirty-third Street had already been plowed by the sanitation crews, who had been busy hitting midtown in the early morning hours. Driving was slow going around the garment district with truckers and their helpers paving a driveway toward the loading dock, snarling traffic for blocks, and angry motorists with hands on horns protesting the triple-parked trucks. A block away on Thirty-fourth Street, decorators for Macy's Department Store were preparing for another busy day.

Inside Rescue Company One, the morning crew had reported on time, all accounted for. The garage door housing the 1959 Mack truck was left open to the curious passersby glancing inside the massive warehouse of the fire department. The twelve firemen were given their duties by their superior, Lieutenant Gerus. On the agenda for the day was the decorating of the firehouse and its six-foot Christmas tree. Part of the crew was left with the task of cleaning the house dorm that housed the crew on duty. The night shift, when not on call, was usually busy studying for promotional exams, while others tried to catch a wink of sleep. In New York, the Fire

Department, along with New York Police, held open houses for the needy in their communities. They would volunteer their time to gather toys given to them by the locals or as donations from the local department stores. Each had their own Santa. In Rescue One, the movement was gathering momentum as toys filled the corner of the firehouse. A Christmas tree had been donated by a local department store, and they even sent their own crew to deliver the tree. Macys had also lent a hand in supplying stuffed animals and dolls to the boys and girls in the Westside area. Still arguing about the noise created by Joe in the morning, Paul heard his name shouted across the cold stationhouse. It was his lieutenant, motioning to Paul to come into the manned office of the firehouse.

Rolling his eyes at Joe, Paul said, "I wonder what he wants now?"

Joe responded, with a grin, "If it's the Christmas tree, tell him to get his behind out from the cozy office and help us."

"You tell him, 'aren't you the one with all the racket?'"

Approaching the office, Lieutenant Gerus said, "It's your boy, Gary, he's on the line."

"Thanks boss," said Paul.

"Hi Daddy."

"Gary, son, I'm sorry for not calling you. I became so occupied with this Christmas tree that I forgot to call my baby."

"Hey Dad, any action today?"

"No, no action. The only action I'll probably see is a bulb falling off the tree. Where's Mommy?"

"Mommy's feeding Christine. You know how she gets if food isn't given to her on time."

"Yeah, I know, son, but remember she's your sister, okay?"

"I know, Daddy, I gotta go. Oh, Daddy, call me if you see any action, okay?"

"Okay, Gary, I'll call you. Tell Mommy I said hello."

Paul could hear Gary screaming just as he hung up, "Mommy, Dad says hello!"

Walking back toward Joe, Paul wondered if today was going to be a calm one. He sure hoped so, because it was cold out there.

"Everything all right?" said Joe.

"Yeah, it was Gary. You know I always call when I arrive. I forgot today, so he called me. He told me if there was any action to call him. That kid loves action."

Joe replied, "I betcha he's going to be just like his dad, a fireman."

"Not if his mother has her way," Paul said.

"Well, buddy," said Joe, "might as well settle in and start decorating this tree before the lieutenant says something."

Looking out to the street through the overhead doors, Paul said, "It's cold out there, Joe. I'd rather be here inside where it's warm. I hope I see no action. Let's do it. Let's get this tree up and running."

Sterling Place
An Abandoned Building
10:00 a.m.

Pulling up to Sterling Place, the two cousins, exhausted and hungry, had finally arrived. Jumping out of the truck, Joe, pointing at the trees that were tied to the back, instructed John to start unloading them; he was headed to the landlord to advise him that he was about to set up shop alongside his abandoned building and to take a much-needed piss. In the middle of the street, Sun Young Lee, a Chinese immigrant who owned a store where he washed and ironed shirts for the neighborhood community, was also busy shoveling his share of the sidewalk in Sterling Place. Sharing the abandoned building with construction workers who were about to start tearing out the inside of the gutted building, John patiently unloaded the trees, resting them against the wall while he waited for Joe to return. The smell of burned wood still left a stench in the area. Six months ago the place went up in smoke in what was called a suspicious fire. The fire had spread over to the next two buildings. Although no one was hurt, property and personal mementos were destroyed. Exiting from next door, Joe, with a thermos filled with coffee, called out to his young nephew. "John, I got some coffee, have some while I finish unloading. I just sold our first tree to Ms. Petigano. Our first sale!"

Joe got permission to get a metal garbage barrel from the inside of the abandoned building. They would need it as the temperature dropped and freezing rain set in. John, with bell in hand, started shouting, "Christmas trees for seven dollars, come get your tree here, Christmas trees seven dollars."

TWA Flight 266
Over Selinsgrove, PA
Seventeen thousand feet
10:05 a.m.

"TWA Flight 266, New York air traffic control is with you, radar checked, confirm requesting altitude."

"Roger, New York, TWA 266 level and maintaining seventeen thousand feet."

"Roger, 266, checked at seventeen thousand. Climb nineteen thousand, maintain nineteen. Advise when flight level has been maintained."

Gusting winds with wet snow were now starting to reappear as the old Constellation with its forty-four occupants was reaching its altitude assigned by New York Center. Captain Wollam didn't understand the change in altitude and didn't bother to question the reason. His cold was now reaching a mild fever, which wasn't good and was noticeable among his two officers. His cold had begun early in the morning in Dayton, Ohio, where his day started, and the rain at four in the morning had left his body in a chill, his bones aching, unable to combat the germs invading his body. Flying was his lifelong dream, though, and a mild cold certainly wasn't going to stop his performance as a pilot and captain as he lifted the nose of the Connie. Meanwhile, in the back cabin, Vincent Flood was sound asleep when he felt gentle hands wrapping a blanket over his chest. Startled, he rose to a sitting position, bumping his forehead with Patricia Post's.

"Oh god, I'm so sorry. Did I hurt you, miss?" said Vincent, rubbing his forehead dazedly.

Sitting next to him on the empty seat, Patricia took a moment to relax her feet. Her early morning route, combined with the bitter weather, had her body aching all over. Being the newest member of the crew, Patty was trying to fulfill her duties as flight attendant. She knew that there would be times when situations like this would come into play. Born and raised in Pennsylvania, Patricia, age twenty, knew that she was born to be in the air. Her refreshing smile was memorable among the crew and to everyone who knew her. Her orders had just come in, and excitement about her promotion into the new jet era had her reeling with joy. Her itinerary, provided by TWA, had her reporting to the company training center in Kansas City, Missouri. This was to be her last flight.

Across the aisle, Arthur Swenson was recovering from the upset stomach that had had him running to the bathroom moments earlier. His symptoms were mainly due to the stress he had gone through while preparing the bid, which was handed to the government by Pratt and Whitney in East Hartford, Connecticut. He, like Captain Wollam, was also coming down with a mild case of the flu. Sipping on ginger ale, suggested by Patricia, Arthur was going through his paperwork when a sharp jolt rattled the plane, sending his plastic cup of ginger ale into the middle of the aisle. Within minutes, the peaceful passengers, who had finally settled in, were up, feeling a sense of anxiety. Both Patricia and Margaret were trying to reassure the passengers that everything was all right. On the deck, Captain Wollam and his crew were busy adjusting the throttle to compensate for the loss of altitude, caused by an air pocket they had encountered. The jolt was so severe that it ripped trays from their settings, throwing them from the small kitchen into the cabin. A brief sound from one of the engines led passengers and the two hostesses to believe that something was wrong. Within minutes, the captain came on the loudspeaker centered in the middle of the cabin with words of assurance.

"Ladies and gentlemen, this is your captain speaking. We're encountering a little turbulence. There is no reason to be alarmed. I will be sending my flight engineer Mr. Rosenthal to do an inspection of the exterior leading to the cabin, just as a precaution. Again, there is no reason to be concerned. Thank you."

Within a minute, First Officer Rosenthal was seen, flashlight in hand, examining the walls to the plane, but what he was really checking was the wings that carried the engines. As every pilot knows, a heavy pocket could damage a wing or even detach an engine, critical in flight to any aircraft. Finding nothing wrong with the plane, the flight engineer headed back to the cockpit. The two pilots were getting ready to descend to eleven thousand feet as instructed by New York control. Looking out the cockpit window, there was no sign of land or sky. TWA 266 was engulfed in a mass of clouds. Control center had advised them that massive clouds were ranging from five hundred feet to eighteen thousand feet. Captain Wollam instructed his crew to be on high alert, for they would be flying solely by instrument. His fear was that there might be traffic in the vicinity.

United Flight 826
Over Allentown, PA.
Twenty-five thousand feet
10:15 a.m.

The faint sound of the four jet engines seemed far away as the whisper liner made its way toward its destination, New York's Idlewild International Airport, at twenty-five thousand feet. Inside the cabin, there was joy and laughter as passengers and crew members interacted with each other over Christmas plans. United 826 had been airborne a little over an hour and the weather that had hampered Chicago was now behind Flight 826; however, the second VOR was still inoperable. Heading closer toward the New York vicinity, the crew took notice of the blinding snowfall that had come from the north. They also noticed that visibility was closing in. It was like looking at a blank wall, seeing nothing.

The best thing about flying is that on those short trips you get to meet fascinating people from all walks of life. Intriguing stories are exchanged among acquaintances of mere hours. Christmas aboard a plane is even more fun; everyone is so kind and humble; it's as if you were actually in heaven.

"New York Center, United Flight 826, with you over Allentown, direct to Idlewild."

"United Flight 826, New York Center clears you to Preston Intersection via Vector 123, please advise present altitude, over."

"Roger, center, 826 altitude 25 thou, please advise New York weather and runway in use, over."

"United 826, New York Center. Idlewild weather is fifteen hundred feet overcast; half mile, light rain with fog, altimeter setting 29.65 runway four left."

With his flight manual in hand, Richard Prewitt was busy going through the jet's panel diagram. It had been over twenty-five minutes and he still had no explanation as to why the second VOR stopped functioning. Flying in zero visibility, the crew was worried about traffic in the area and the hazardous environment surrounding United 826. In the cabin, two individuals who had met just under an hour earlier had become friends. Darnell and Steven were busy chatting about their Christmases and who they were spending it with. Darnell had told his eleven-year-old friend about the great game that he had participated in on the campus court at the University of Omaha. He had also told him stories about Alabama, where he was born, and Summit, New Jersey, where he was raised. Intrigued, the kid kept asking him questions. The youngster, Darnell noticed, was not afraid to talk to him. Steven viewed his older friend as another person, and the color of his skin didn't affect his politeness. Little Stevie had mentioned that he was flying alone and admitted that he was a little scared, especially since he couldn't see the ground below him . . .

Raised in a religious and loving family, Darnell knew that his little friend was indeed scared, and opted to put away the books to chat with the lonely boy. He was especially touched when the red-haired boy asked him if he would stay with him until his mother and sister arrived for him. With a warm and reassuring smile, Darnell wrapped his arm around the kid with a big heart, and assured him that no matter he would stay until Mommy arrived. Almost instantly, the little boy placed his head against the young man's arm who had taken the responsibility to care for him.

"Okay, Richard," said Captain Sawyer, "let's call the company, and advise them that the VOR is down. I don't see any solution to this."

Sleeting rain was starting to stick to the cockpit window, a sight not liked by the crew of Flight 826.

"United Com. Flight 826 advising default instrument, requesting inspection upon landing, over."

"Roger, 826, United Com, message understood, advise the instrument in question, over."

"United Com, second VOR nonoperable, no sign of recovering in flight."

"Roger, 826, copy that, report to warehouse terminal upon arrival to Idlewild, good day."

"Skipper," a worried first officer said, "should we notify New York Center?"

Looking out his left window, Captain Sawyer contemplated the question asked by his right-hand man, turned toward him, and with no sign of concern, said, "No, Bobby, I don't consider this an emergency, do you?"

TWA Flight 266
Passing Allentown, PA
Eleven thousand feet
10:21:23 a.m.

With less than forty minutes remaining in flight, TWA 266 was now preparing for its final stage of descent into the New York area. The soon-to-be-replaced Constellation was performing efficiently with operational conditions, according to data obtained from Second Officer Leroy Rosenthal, who had just finished inspecting the inner frame after the severe jolt that had shaken the entire plane and its passengers. Waiting for instructions from New York Center to start down, Captain Wollam was perhaps the most in need of landing his fever had risen and his shirt was soaked with perspiration from the flu. His only comfort was knowing that his wife, Nanette, would be picking him up at the terminal. He kept thinking to himself that the flight wasn't as depressing as his cold was. Flying the old horse wasn't so bad; he felt a connection between the Connie and himself. He had nicknamed her Betsy, and he would talk to her during difficult times.

Betsy was the kind of plane any pilot dreamed of flying in the '50s. Reaching 133 feet in length, the model plane was first introduced to the public in 1950. The instruments of the prop plane were those of simplicity in arrangement, making it a wonder for the passengers as well as the crew, but modern technology and the jet era forced the Constellation to take a backseat. Captain Wollam was used to this kind of weather; worries of blinding snow didn't bother him; his plane flew well under such conditions. Perspiration shining his forehead even while he maintained his composure, the skipper asked his first officer for the cruise descent checklist. The crew knew the captain and his capabilities under such strain, and they had no concern about his accelerating cold, affecting his flight performance.

"New York Center, TWA 266 passing Allentown at eleven thousand feet, frequency 125.3 inbound to LaGuardia. Standing by for letdown." Pause.

"TWA 266, you're breaking up, say again. Are you leaving eleven or maintaining eleven?"

"New York Center, TWA 266 maintaining eleven thousand feet, ready to start descent toward New York LaGuardia."

"TWA 266, New York Center, copy that 266. New York Center has you on radar, advise current LaGuardia weather: Measured five hundred overcast, one mile visibility in light snow, surface wind northwest fifteen knots, altimeter setting 29.66. Stand by to copy."

"Roger, New York Center, TWA 266 acknowledge that, standing by."

Knowing that within minutes he, his crew, and his passengers would be on solid ground, Captain Wollam seemed a little more settled in his seat, ready for their final descent into the Linden holding pattern over New Jersey. By now, winds had picked up as David Wollam tried to maintain the flight level. The vibrations in the pilot's yoke (stick) were noticeable as the auto-pilot was disengaged.

"TWA 266, New York Center clears you for letdown into Jersey, Linden Intersection. Descend to nine thousand and maintain altitude and heading. Weather advisory remains same, overcast five hundred, one mile visibility in light snow, possible freezing rain, surface winds fifteen miles northwest, altimeter steady setting at 29.66. Center advised Instrument Landing System (ILS) approaches being made to runway four. TWA please be advised that localizer is inoperative."

"New York Center, TWA 266, roger that, we're leaving eleven for nine, maintain level flight and heading."

Throttling down to cruise descent, 266 was now twenty minutes from landing, the instruments were all operable, and the four engines responding to the captain's command. The crew had noticed that the snow was not light, as stated, but rather blinding. The crew was now depending on their instruments and New York Center.

United Flight 826
Approaching New Jersey
Twenty-five thousand feet
10:21:32 a.m.

Above the light snowstorm gripping the entire East Coast, United 826 was cruising comfortably toward Idlewild. The clear blue sky above them showed no evidence of the mess that lay below. Captain Sawyer and his crew knew that it was only a matter of time before they were given instructions by the New York Center for a standard cruise descent into the New Jersey area. Knowing what they were in for, Robert Sawyer wanted to get as close as possible to the Preston Intersection area without losing his present altitude. His experience heading into Chicago earlier that morning had left him a bit on edge. He kept thinking of the difficulties he and his crew had endured trying to navigate in the dense fog and he did not wish to repeat it.

But now, Captain Sawyer had a decision to make on the defective number two VOR. It had been over half an hour since Richard Prewitt his second officer, had tried in vain to get the needle of the VOR operable. There was no evidence of blown fuses or burned wires; his analyses of the DC-8 panel showed that the probable cause was most likely a frozen needle. If so, then there was nothing he could do.

"Bobby, call aeronautical radio communication again, advise them of our situation, advise them that we're on course and on time to Idlewild. I want to make sure they fix the darned thing before we leave on Sunday."

"Will do, Skipper. What about Idlewild, should I also advise on the down VOR?"

"No, Bobby, not yet. I don't anticipate a problem in our letdown into Preston. We'll wait until we reach Preston, and we'll see then, okay?"

The transmission had been sent as requested by the captain, and now it was up to United Home Base to relay the message to New York's headquarters based at Idlewild.

Tucked safely into his seat and surrounded by two warm blankets, little Steven Baltz, his face a picture of innocence, was sound asleep. The little boy had been up since five that morning. Unable to sleep the night before from all the excitement, Steven just plain dozed off in the middle of a sentence. His new friend Darnell was sitting across from him, glancing into the open space outside his window, his thoughts on his family and friends in Summit, New Jersey. Unable to study as he had promised himself he would, Darnell adjusted his little red-haired friend's blanket. He had amazed Darnell with his knowledge and wisdom at such a young age. Knowing very well that he and his little friend would part ways upon arriving in New York and probably never see each other again, Darnell wanted to give the feisty kid a Christmas present, but all he had was the T-shirt that he had promised his younger brother Johnny. Wanting to keep his promise, he removed the university baseball cap he had worn for the trip and placed it on the little boy's head as a token of friendship.

"United 826, New York Center. Roger, we have your progress. Advise radar service not available at this time. Clear to Preston Intersection, via Jet Route 60 direct to Robbinsville, via Vector 123 to Preston. Clear to descend to thirteen thousand feet, maintain thirteen thousand feet. Advise when established."

"New York Center, United 826, sir, we'd rather hold upstairs, over."

"United 826, New York Center, copy that." Pause. "826, switch frequencies to different controller at 123.6; you'll still be with New York Center."

Coming on the heels of his words of defiance, Robert Sawyer knew that the sudden change in controller meant that he and New York Center would have a side debate on separate channels. "Why would they switch on me?" he thought. Nevertheless, the skipper was determined to maintain his present altitude for as long as possible, for him and the people that he was responsible for. Sawyer knew that there were two small problems involved in a letdown under such conditions. The first was what the controller had said: "Radar not available" That meant that 826 would be doing their own navigation while they descended through blinding snow. Second, they would be flying with only one VOR into solid fog, and possibly with other traffic as well.

"New York Center, United 826 with you on 123.6. We're cleared to thirteen thousand to maintain twenty-five thousand until we had conversation with you. If we're going to have a delay, we would rather hold upstairs than down. We're going to need three-fourths of a mile to Idlewild, do you have weather handy?"

"No, but I'll get it for you. I show no delays until now, 826. I could clear you to Preston via Victor 30 until you intercept Victor 123 that way to Preston. It'll be a little bit quicker, approximately eleven miles. Weather to Idlewild fifteen hundred feet overcast, half-mile light rain, fog altimeter setting 29.65. We still show no delays, you're actually number one."

Pause. "Ok, Center, will start down to thirteen thousand feet."

"Roger, 826, sorry to break you up, make it eleven thousand, repeat eleven thousand."

"Center, this is 826 leaving 25 thou starting descent to eleven. See you then."

TWA 266
Nine thousand feet
Inbound to Linden, New Jersey
10:29:49 a.m.

"New York Center, TWA 266 passing Solberg, VOR, leveling off at nine thousand feet."

"Roger that 266. New York Center with you, please be advised that radar is terminated, contact LaGuardia Approach Control on 125.7. Good day."

With minutes left to touchdown, 266 was now smack in the middle of a blinding snowfall carrying with it heavy fog and shifting rain. The rays of bright sun coming from the east made the descent more blinding, and more dangerous. Inside the cabin, all was quiet as passengers prepared to gather their belongings. The two young stewardesses had secured the small kitchen in the forward part of the plane. The long journey was now coming to an end for most, but for Vincent Flood, who had succumbed to a lapsing deep sleep, it was just the beginning.

His dream took him into a place he'd never seen before. In his dream, it was late evening, except that in this dream, everything was a grayish black. He felt scared, trapped, and hopeless, and yet for reasons unknown, he felt compelled to stay there. His dream took him to an old country dirt road adjoining what seemed to be a farm. A worn-out barn stood at his left, and he noticed that the farm had no animals, nor did it have any occupants. He remembered taking this dirt road before, a short cut to his house a couple of miles down, he just didn't know when. He knew that he was heading home, but didn't know why he had left there in the first place. Following the dirt road, he came upon something that wasn't there before, something that terrified him, something that made him gasp for air in his sleep. He turned to get away from the horrible image that was in front of him but he felt a jerk, holding him back as he tried to rip away from the vise that claimed him. The yanks started getting rougher, his heart beating faster.

"Excuse me, sir, sorry that I had to tug on you to wake you, but you have to start buckling up, captain's order."

Startled, Vincent was more than happy that Patricia Post had nudged him, helping him escape from the nightmare that had left him drenched and weary. Still groggy from sleep, the young man rubbed his eyes to restore his vision as he looked outside the cabin window. He noticed that the weather had worsened.

Trying to get a fix on the ground below, Vincent lurched up from his seat to get a clear view of a vertical hole in the clouds that shed a glimpse of the terrain below. Suddenly, he was jerked backward into his seat by a sudden drop in altitude. The Constellation was now in the final stages for letdown, visibility at a standstill and winds rocking the aircraft. With his dream still fresh in his mind, Vincent's drawn reflection caught Patty's attention. With no time to take her station, Patty had decided to sit next to the sleepy and confused boy.

"Sorry to interrupt," she said to the young man next to her. "Are you all right? You look confused. Is there anything I can do for you?"

"No, thank you, it's just that I had a bad dream. Thanks for waking me up—the timing was perfect."

"Perfect? I don't understand," Patty said with a look of concern and a smile of gratitude.

"I had this dream that I was on a farm. The place looked so spooky, and it was so real. I felt as if I had been there before, but I couldn't remember when. Anyway, I came upon this scene; it was horrible, something had come down from the sky. I couldn't make out what it was, but there were a lot of burned and torn trees, most still on fire. There were bodies all over the field. The barn had caught fire and the grass next to the dirt road was also burning. And then there it was, right in front of me." His voice trailed off.

The young and pretty stewardess sat there silently. What could she say? She didn't know him. All she knew was that he was a passenger by the name of Vincent Flood. Looking at him, she saw this young, lost man, needing reassurance. She felt compelled to ask him, "Vincent, what did you see?"

Bowing his head in frustration, with hands clenched and knees trembling, he said, "I saw myself among the ruins. At first, I thought it was somebody else, but then the strangest thing happened. He or me rose from the ashes and pointed straight at me. My heart wanted to rip away from my chest. He was crying. Wiping his tears from his eyes, he turned and started to walk to a forklike road. The one on the right was bright and had trees that weren't burned. They had fruit, and the road was paved. The other road was dark and gray, the twigs on the trees were black and burned, and there was no life down that road. He, or I, had to choose which road to take. He was about to choose when you woke me up. I guess I'll never know."

"Well, I hope I didn't ruin the suspense, Vincent. What do you think it meant?"

"I don't know, but it seemed so real. Anyway, thanks again for waking me up. I didn't want to know which one he took. Or should I say, which one I took."

United 826
Inbound to Preston
Fourteen thousand feet
10:30:07 a.m.

"United 826, New York Center, I show you crossing the centerline Vector 30 at this time, please confirm."

"Roger, New York Center, United 826, good to hear from you. Roger that. 826 confirm established on Vector 30, requesting distance from Vector 123 by way of Preston."

"Roger, 826, New York Center shows you fifteen, now make it sixteen miles for Vector 123. Right now New York Center shows you about two miles from crossing Vector 433. Stand by to copy."

"Standing by, 826."

The elegant new jetliner was on its cruise descent and the quiet engines were humming, a faint sound that brought a sense of relief to the occupants inside. By now, all was hushed as passengers, anxious to get their feet on solid ground, kept to themselves. As far as the seventy-seven passengers and the four stewardesses were concerned, the flight was normal. The furious weather had tested the capability of the jet, and everyone was satisfied with the performance of the crew and the machine. Its comfort was never an issue. However, inside the cockpit, the crew of Flight 826 was now engaged in a more serious problem. Without visual reference to the ground and a down VOR, Captain Sawyer and his two men knew that Preston was dead ahead, but they didn't know how far. The view from the cockpit was at zero visibility as the wipers struggled to eradicate the wet snow that slithered across the windshield.

In perspective, the crew was acting in accordance with the rules of the New York Center, as they were the eyes of Flight 826. With charts in his lap, Robert Fiebling was determining the position of the plane in line with the intersection. A fix from the surviving VOR established them nine minutes to Preston, at current speed and descent.

"United 826, New York Center. Cleared to descend to and maintain five thousand feet, turn right heading zero-four-five degrees. Looks like you'll be able to make Preston at five thousand in time. We show leaving fourteen thousand feet, confirm." over.

"Roger, Center, 826 leaving fourteen thousand for five thousand, we'll try to make Preston on time."

"Roger, 826, New York Center. If holding is necessary at Preston, go southwest one minute, pattern right turns, the only delay I show will be in your descent into Preston."

"Copy that, Center. 826, no delays, thank you."

Inside, the three men with their crisp clean white shirts were feeling a sense of hesitation as they silently watched the little gauge that told them their altitude was slowly dropping. The silence broke when Richard Prewitt asked a simple question. "Hey, boss, when are we going to Macy's?"

"Well, Richard, first I want to land this plane, then I want to get to my hotel and have a nice hot bath. Then we'll see about Macy's. First things first, and right now we have to get this plane to five thousand feet, which brings me to another question, any luck on the down VOR?"

"No, skipper, might as well forget number two, it's dead."

"Okay, gents, let's concentrate on our letdown. We need to make Preston at five thousand feet and we have sixteen miles before Preston, so let's stay alert. All we have is another twenty minutes of flying time, and then back to sunny California in two days."

TWA 266
Approaching Linden
Passing eight thousand feet
10:30:49 a.m.

"TWA Flight 266, this is LaGuardia approach control, reduce to approach speed, clear to descend to five thousand feet, maintain five thousand, maintain heading, confirm at five." over.

"Roger, LaGuardia, 266 leaving eight for five, reducing to approach speed."

Looking out the window, Captain David Wollam noticed that the snow was turning to freezing rain, the evidence on the windshield in front of him as the wipers removed the splattered snow, pushing it to the sides. With zero visibility, the captain and his crew knew that they were in for twenty-five minutes of hellish weather. He and his crew had years of flight training for such conditions and today was no different. Feeling a little better from his cold, Captain Wollam was now settling back in his chair, the very same chair that he had occupied for the past three years.

Everyone aboard was feeling the burden of the early flight, especially Juanita Mullins. She had risen very early to prepare her infant son for the long and cold trip. Her husband Cecil had not been much help, he was nursing a wicked cold, and all he had in mind was sunny Puerto Rico, where they would be in about four hours.

Just three rows down sat Vincent Flood, by now Vincent had settled back, his nightmare behind him. He had thanked Patty for her encouragement and understanding. Looking out the window, he could see patches of land through the clouds; the sun was penetrating the clouds as it rose from the east, and New York was coming into view. A bluish line streaked across the atmosphere, resembling a rainbow, perhaps a sign of a beautiful and blessed day.

"TWA 266, this is LaGuardia approach control. Sir, what is your altitude?"

"LaGuardia approach control, this is TWA Flight 266, we're leaving sixty-five hundred for five thousand."

"Roger that, TWA 266, this is approach control. Turn right to a heading of 130 degrees, please advise when reaching five thousand, heading 130." over.

"Roger, control tower. TWA 266 turning right heading 130, will call you at five thousand."

"Hey Dean, how about putting up those wipers a little higher?"

"Skipper, they're at maximum now."

"Let's stay alert, boys, we're flying blind for the next twenty minutes. I'll buy breakfast for the first one that sees land."

Sterling Place
Brooklyn, New York
10:32:12 a.m.

News of the cousins' little venture had hit the community of Seventh Avenue and Sterling Place. Within an hour, the cousins had sold more than ten trees and were very happy with their progress. With fire from a garbage can to keep them warm, Joseph and John had big smiles on their faces despite the bitter cold. The boys were well known in the community, and everyone who knew them was contributing to their venture. Joseph figured that the way it was going, they would be sold out by two o' clock that afternoon. If so, that meant that they would have to be up very early again the next morning to make the same trip to New Jersey to get fifty more trees, if not more. He also felt that if he made a trip to New Jersey every day it would ruin his pocket, giving less profit to him and Joseph. He needed to talk to the landlord who was kind enough to let them use the vacant building, to see if it was possible for him to keep the trees inside overnight. That way, he would not have to make a trip every day to New Jersey; instead, he'd buy 150 trees and keep them in the burned-out building. If they only sold fifty trees per day, within nine days they would have sold more than 450, giving them a substantial profit. So far the plan had worked. Joseph had finally come up with a winner. Looking over his right shoulder, he could see John huddling around the garbage can that kept them warm. The weather had started to pick up and the snow had gradually turned to freezing rain, making it a bit colder than they had anticipated. Smiling, John walked over to Joseph and hugged him, saying, "Cousin, we're going to get rich out of this new adventure you created. I'm going to get some coffee, do you want some?"

"Sure, I could use some right about now. It's getting colder out here by the minute."

"I'll be right back."

"Hurry back, John, it might get busy in a little while."

United Flight 826
Approaching Preston
Seven thousand feet
10:33:21 a.m.

"United 826, this is New York Center, how do you read? Over."

"Roger, Center, 826 reading you loud and clear."

"826, New York Center, can you please give status?"

"New York Center, 826 United leaving seven thousand, inbound to Preston. Destination Idlewild, can you give us weather conditions and active runway?"

"Roger, 826, New York Center, stand by."

The weather was starting to pick up as the huge jet bounced around the atmosphere like a helplessly dangling kite, waiting to come down. Inside the cabin, the seventy-seven passengers and four stewardesses prepared for landing. With the exception of the stewardesses, each passenger was buckled in. They were moments away from meeting their loved ones at the airport. The flight attendants were likewise happy with the way the flight had gone. There was no sign of land yet out the cabin window. Instead, white clouds surrounded the aircraft, but they could feel by the vibration of the aircraft that they were on the descent to Idlewild.

In the middle of the cabin seated to the right, Darnell Mallory was busy packing his school books. Seated across from him was little Stephen Baltz, wearing the big baseball cap that Darnell had given him. He was awakened by Patricia Keller, one of the flight attendants, as he needed to be in an upright position to buckle up. Looking out his window, Stephen was surprised that there was still no land in sight. Looking worried, Steven turned to Darnell and said, "Are we there yet, Mr. Darnell?" "Not yet," replied Darnell. "We're about five minutes away, then you can see your mom and sister. How is that, little buddy?"

"Do you think that Mommy and my sister Randee are there already?"

"I think so, but if they're not, I promised you I'd wait with you until they get there, okay?"

Concern fading from his face, Stephen replied, "Ok, Darnell."

"United 826, this is New York Center. Weather advisory fifteen hundred feet, overcast half mile, light rain. Be advised of fog in the area, altimeter settings 29.65, active runway is four left, no delays. The only delay will be your descent, over."

"Roger, New York, United 826 copy that. No delays here, we're out of seven for six."

"Roger, 826. You're breaking up, did you say leaving six?"

"826 is leaving seven for six."

"Roger, 826 leaving seven for six. 826 you have received holding instructions for Preston. Radar service is now terminated, please contact Idlewild Approach Control. Good day."

"Thank you, New York Center. 826, good day, and Merry Christmas."

"Roger, 826, New York Center, Merry Christmas to you, too, sir."

In the cockpit, the crew of Flight 826 was busy preparing for the letdown into Idlewild Airport. Their main concern now was navigating through the thick white clouds that blinded them, making it difficult for them to make visual contact with the ground below.

Each member of the flight crew was occupied with his or her own tasks, reassuring themselves of a safe descent into the Metropolitan area. Captain Sawyer was focused on flying his aircraft while his first officer, scanned the atmosphere for any sign of land or traffic. His second officer was also placed on high alert, looking out the captain's window for anything out of the ordinary.

"Robert, give me an ETA to Preston."

"Well, Skipper, it's now ten thirty-three. We should be arriving over Preston at ten thirty-nine."

"Richard, contact Idlewild. Tell them we're at five thousand feet, approaching Preston."

"Idlewild approach control, United 826 approaching Preston at five thousand feet. Over."

Looking out the window into the clouds, Darnell wondered who was picking him up. "Would it be his sister Mordine or his parents?" He knew that the drive from New Jersey would be a difficult one due to the weather, but he hoped somebody was there waiting for him. Looking at the plane's right wing, he noticed that the flaps were coming down, an indication that they were within minutes of landing. The sound of the flaps seemed to disturb the aerodynamics of the plane, and then he heard the landing gears come down. That was scary, as the plane wobbled up and down. Then, within a heartbeat, he saw something that wasn't supposed to be there, something that numbed his entire body, leaving his vocal cords frozen, unable to scream in fear. His heart had been rooted from his chest and was now pushing up his throat, trying to escape his body. Augustine Ferrer saw what he did, and screamed in terror, startling everyone.

Inside the cockpit, the crew had also seen what the passengers were now witnessing. Suddenly, it was there, without warning, and the screams of fear from the cabin were heard in the cockpit.

"Oh my God, someone yelled. We're going to die!"

The chilling words came from Robert Fiebling as he stared at the massive object that emerged from the clouds, coming into view only a few feet in front of him, with its big red letters: TWA.

"Oh shit!" screamed the captain, his voice uncertain with fear and desperation.

TWA Flight 266
Over Linden, NJ
Five thousand feet
10:33:28 a.m.

"TWA Flight 266, LaGuardia approach control has you on radar, over."

"Roger, LaGuardia Approach, TWA Flight 266 is with you, radar established."

"Roger, 266, LaGuardia approach control copy that. 266, you're number one to land, visibility half mile, heavy fog in area, surface winds fifteen miles at 230 degrees, runway in use twenty-two left, I show no delay."

"Copy that LaGuardia, no delays, TWA 266."

"TWA 266, LaGuardia approach advises traffic at two o'clock, six miles northeast-bound heading, do you copy?"

"266, we copy."

There was calm in the cabin as the passengers felt a sense of relief, knowing that they were within minutes of landing. Seated on the left side of the plane, Vincent Flood was anxious to set his feet on solid ground and looking forward to seeing his family. Seated across the aisle from him was Juanita Mullins, preparing her infant son for the cold weather that lay ahead. Seated in back of her was Arthur Swenson, whose upset stomach had followed him from Ohio, but other than that was happy to be home. The only thing on his mind was spending the weekend with his wife and three children in Connecticut and reporting to work on Monday with the new contract.

"TWA 266, LaGuardia approach control, roger that. Appears to be jet traffic off your right, now appears to be at three o' clock, one mile northeast-bound, do you copy? over."

"Roger, LaGuardia approach control. 266 we copy that, traffic off my right."

"Trans-World 266, LaGuardia approach. Turn left, one zero-zero degrees."

Pause. "266, LaGuardia approach, do you copy? TWA 266, I say again, this is LaGuardia approach control, turn left one zero-zero degrees, over. TWA 266, do you copy? TWA 266, do you copy?"

There was no warning. The sleek silver jet rammed into the Constellation with force and vengeance. Within seconds, chaos erupted inside the doomed cabin as the mystery jet tore through the roof of the Constellation, leaving the passengers defenseless, with no shelter from the cold environment outside. Meanwhile, inside the cockpit, the crew tried helplessly to control the condemned aircraft.

The United jet came in on a forty-five degree angle, slicing through the number three and four engines of the Connie, spreading the debris from the blades, which tore into the already maimed fuselage, slicing it in half like butter and instantly detaching it from its frame. A huge turbine jet ripped away the ceiling, swallowing a passenger who was trying to help a confused and desperate woman. He was sucked into the fan blades and the turbine jet coughed out his remains on the other side. The Constellation was breaking up, the structure of the cabin weakened leaving passengers to fight for their lives. The collision seemed to take years even though it had been only seconds, as the huge jet tore through the helpless, destroyed plane. A loud thunder of twisting metal was heard as the plane, or what was left of it, finally broke into three parts.

A horrible scream ripped through the cabin. It was Juanita. Her infant son, who moments before had been secured in her lap, was torn from her grasp. The child twirled in the air toward the ground. Her husband Cecil tried in vain to rescue his son, but it was too late, and as the cold wind poured over him, he was unaware that next to him his wife Juanita had unbuckled her seat belt in a desperate attempt to rescue her son. She was also sucked out of the plane.

Vincent Flood was in the fight of his life. The jet had ripped a huge gash over his seat, leaving him partially dangling in the air, clinging to a strap from his seat belt as the beastly wind wrapped around his body, trying to tear his fingers loose from their grip. Looking up to the sky, he felt a momentary sense of motionless, a sense of tranquility. His life was played back to him in a flash, and he knew then that he would die. He looked to find Patricia, who in next to no time had become his friend. She, too, was missing and, he could only presume, dead. He glanced for a moment at the empty seat that had been occupied by Juanita, and saw her husband weeping with grief and anger, screaming, "They're gone, they're gone!"

And he knew what had happened. Two rows in back of him he saw Arthur Swenson slumped sideways in his seat, a gush of blood coming from his forehead. His notebook was still in his hand, its leaves fluttering back and forth in the chilling wind. The fuselage bent in half, making a horrible sound like that of a rusted metal door being opened. The razor-sharp sheet metal from the condemned plane became a hazard to anyone near it. The sky was visible through the gaping hole above, left by the jet that had dropped out of the sky without warning. Visible hairline fractures on the sides of the fuselage became noticeable as the snow rushed in, slowly breaking up the Constellation, leaving the passengers open to the blistering chill and sucking bodies into the atmosphere, sending them to their deaths. From inside the cockpit, the crew looked on helplessly as the fuselage, with everyone inside, broke away, their screams fading until they could hear no more, cartwheeling into oblivion. There was nothing to do as the three men seated at their stations tumbled toward the earth with only the two remaining engines, still mounted on the surviving wing.

There would be no survivors, and the crew and passengers aboard the ill-fated flight would become another mystery in the annals of aviation investigation. Clearly, Captain David Wollam had piloted his aircraft in accordance with the rules of the Federal Aviation Administration, and he had complied with all the functions required and mandated by his company, the Civil Aeronautics Board, and the FAA. His only mistake was being there at that precise moment and trusting the men who, by all accounts, should have been monitoring traffic along Flight 266's path. I can only imagine what went on inside that plane—the panic, the dreams that were never completed.

TWA—Constellation Structure after Collision

The majority of the collision's force impacting on the Connie was centered around the following points:

The DC-8 entered over the right side of the Constellation on a forty-five degree angle, immediately destroying the number three and four propeller engines. It toppled over the plane like a hungry hawk, swooping down on its prey with force and vengeance as it tore the fuselage with its landing gears and exited through the back, destroying the middle and left rudder tail fin section. The Constellation was left in a heap of rubble. Evidence of the force of impact came in the form of the jet parts that were tangled in the ruin of the Constellation.

The forward section of the passenger compartment between the fuselage and tail section was destroyed. The right vertical fin, rudder, and outboard portion of the right horizontal and twelve-foot stabilizer were torn off. The right wing flap and right aileron were missing.

The aft section, including the empennage, separated from the forward portion of the aircraft. In-flight fire was evidenced by soot and scorching, and evidence of fire on board was found on the bodies of the passengers. The right wing and number four engine separated at the wing section and landed six hundred feet east of the aft fuselage section.

An in-flight explosion in the number four engine was also evident. The number three engine also suffered an explosion while in air and was found six hundred feet northeast of the aft fuselage. The forward section of the fuselage and left wing, including the number one and two engines, impacted approximately one thousand feet north of the aft fuselage.

Numerous pieces of aircraft structure were strewn over a wide area in the vicinity of Miller Field. Many of these pieces were identified as parts of a DC-8. Most of the bodies from the TWA that were ejected from the impact in flight were found several miles from the wreckage.

United 826
After collision
10:33:37 a.m.

The DC-8 shuddered, as the crew inside struggled to maintain the plane's altitude, fighting the controls, trying to untangle the plane from the twisting metal of the Constellation below.

The landing gears of the jet in their down position acted like claws, fracturing the fuselage of the Connie. Without warning or time to react, the United jet swooped down on top of Flight 266, wiping out the number three and four propeller engines, its right wing disengaging from the main frame. Its occupants, jolted but unaware of what had just taken place, screamed in fear. The jet continued on its path of destruction, cutting through the middle and left section of the rudder. It slowly exited, leaving annihilation and death in its path. It disappeared into the blinding clouds just as suddenly as it had appeared.

"Mayday, mayday, this is United Flight 826, we have collided with what appears to be a Constellation airplane. Mayday, mayday, this is United Flight 826, we have collided with what seems to be a Constellation airplane, come in, over. Captain, the radio isn't working. The antennas must have been destroyed in the collision."

"Richard, check the luggage compartment below and see what kind of damage we have. Oh my God, Robert, what the hell happened?"

The words came from the dazed and concerned captain as he desperately held onto the yoke of the plane, trying to control the force of the impact. The yoke was rattling back and forth in his hands. His left cheek was swollen from flying debris.

By now, the cabin was in disarray as terrified passengers witnessing the scene outside their windows screamed in fear and disbelief. Warning bells rang inside the cockpit, one of them telling the pilots that a stall was imminent. That sound terrifies any pilot. The stunned flight engineer slowly opened the so-called basement door. Cold air rushed in and he reacted immediately and instinctively, closing it. Passengers looked on in mingled hope and fear as the second officer rushed by. Parts of the nose of the plane were torn off and the windshield cracked, shattered glass flying into the cockpit where the three men struggled to keep the plane in the air long enough to land at Idlewild. In the cabin, where moments before there had been laughter and happiness, there was now confusion, fear, and chaos.

"Captain, number four engine is gone, and we lost three and two, number one is losing pressure."

"Robert, we're never going to make it to Idlewild. We have no ailerons or rudder. I can't turn the controls are not responding."

"Captain, there's a park over there, straight ahead."

"It doesn't matter where we land," the captain said. "It's going to be catastrophic. Give me altitude, Robert, what's our altitude?"

"Skipper, we're at three thousand and dropping five hundred feet per minute. Oh my God, we're not going to make it. We're coming down hard on a populated area. This doesn't look good."

Fear and anguish in his eyes, Richard Prewitt approached the captain. The prognosis didn't look promising. The baggage compartment below had suffered substantial damage; the ground could be seen through the huge gap. The structures of the landing gear had been twisted and bent. The four wheels on one of the back structures were missing, and the front nose was nowhere to be seen. Parts of the metal frame were dangling, the wind twisting it back and forth. The sound of a dog locked up in a cage, howling with fear, calling for its master, came from below. The sluggish plane veered sideways, trembling and losing altitude. It dropped like a lead sinker, its controls inoperable.

The undercarriage of the plane was totally gutted, the communications were wiped out, and the silver right wing had a ten-degree downward bend, causing the aircraft to become unbalanced. Sparks were coming out of the pod of the number four engine, and the number three dangled, held on only by the last two bolts of the frame. Smoke filled the entire cabin, and everyone was stricken with panic. In one corner in the back of the plane, little Stephen Baltz bent his knees to his chest and buried his face, crying as he tried to hide himself from the confusion surrounding him. The screams were agonizing, everyone's eyes glued to the windows leading to the outside world, as the crippled plane crossed the Hudson River. They could see the buildings on the other side, and they could see the cars becoming bigger and bigger, an indication that they were losing altitude rapidly. A humming sound came from the plane's only surviving engine, flickering on and off, threatening to flame off completely. Darnell saw that Stephen was crying hysterically and rushed to him. Trying to keep his balance, he reached the confused and frightened kid and wrapped his arms around him, sheltering him from the tangled and shattered jet.

Footnote*

In order for an aircraft of any size to stay airborne, it must coordinate with four forces (Lift, Thrust, Gravity, and Drag). For the plane to stay airborne, Lift must be greater than Gravity, and Thrust must be greater than Drag.

Captain Sawyer and his two crewmen fought the elements of flight, but it was a losing battle. The wind prowling the deck made it more difficult for the crew inside to control the flight. They were now on a slow descending course, their speed still too fast to land on any possible terrain other than an airport runway. The captain tried in vain to hold the nose up, preventing the plane from going into a nosedive, but feared it might go into a spiral dive if it stalled. As they approached the borough of Brooklyn, screams of fear and shock echoed through the cabin, passengers huddling with each other for comfort and guidance, prayers rising through the screams.

The man in command, his eyes a little watery, turned to his friend and first officer and said, "Robert, oh my God, I'm so sorry. What are my three girls going to say?"

"Captain, we're gonna make it. We're gonna make it." The words were of a desperate copilot.

"No, friend, that down there is concrete. We're not making the park."

Suddenly, there was a loud hum from the number one engine. The turbine was on its last breath as it fluttered on and off like Morse code, an indication that a flameout was imminent. In the cabin the four flight stewardesses, Mary, Augustine, Annie, and Patricia, raced up and down the aisle trying to maintain calm among the confused and disoriented passengers. The smoke combined with the smell of ruptured fuel made it difficult to breath, causing even more panic. Some had gone into shock; they just sat in their seats, staring out the window as the view of Brooklyn below became bigger and bigger. Other passengers sought answers from the four stewardesses, who knew that the prognosis wasn't too favorable.

Outside the window, the right wing was missing an engine, and if you looked closer you could see that the flap and aileron were missing and the leading edge was bent. Flames were building and beginning to slip upward from what was left of the luggage compartment below, and the crew feared an explosion from the ruptured fuel lines. One spark in the right place could start a chain reaction, causing a breech in the power plant. Although from the inside, the plane didn't look too bad, on the outside it was obvious that the jet was heavily damaged.

In the cockpit, every sentence had to be screamed over to the high-pitched wind coming through the broken windshield. It was now do or die, as the trio struggled with the out-of-control plane.

"Richard, give me the status on the engines. Tell me what I have left, Richard!"

"Skipper, there's nothing left. What you're hearing is the humming of the fan blade of engine number one; it's dying. There it goes, Skipper, shutting down engine one. We're now in a glide."

"Robert!" screamed the captain. "Give me left hard rudder! What's my altitude?"

"We're dropping fast! Bobby, you gotta stretch it a little longer. Stretch it, damn it! We're at seven hundred feet you gotta keep it flying for a little longer, Captain."

"It's too heavy. I have no control. I'm losing control. I can't keep her up."

"You're going to hit the building, Captain! Oh my God! Oh my God!"

"No! No!"

Screams of agony could be heard coming from the back. The eerie sound of dying souls could be heard in the front, but there was nothing that could be done. The eighty-four people aboard could do nothing but sit and wait for impact. It was certain that the plane was heading toward a main street below. Unexpectedly, the plane made first contact with its left wing, clipped a building and spinning it out of control. A loud sound came from below as the plane started to disintegrate. Inside, the sound of twisting metal could be heard as the fuselage crumpled under pressure. In the back, Darnell was trying to comfort Stephen, while looking in horror toward the pavement below. His fear was interrupted when Stephen, with tears in his eyes and an unsteady voice, said, "Darnell, don't leave me, okay? Promise me that you won't leave me."

"Don't worry, buddy," responded Darnell. "I told you that I would stay with you until your mommy and sister arrive. Didn't I say that, huh? Didn't

I?" Knowing what lay ahead, and knowing that it was just a matter of time now, Darnell wrapped his arms around his little friend, sheltering him from the debris that was headed their way. What seemed like minutes was actually seconds as the jet slammed into a house; it bounced off and smashed a lamp pole and utility post, then sideswiped a building as it crashed onto the street below. It raced down the street like a locomotive, out of control. The sheet metal that protected the aircraft was now a deadly weapon as it swirled through the cabin like a ravaging hurricane, its sharp edges cutting through human flesh, mutilating some and decapitating others. Then the tail section ripped off, leaving some of the passengers trapped inside the large fuselage as it rolled down the street, obliterating itself. There was no sound coming from what was left of the inside. All that was left was the embodiment of death.

The DC-8 Structure after the Collision

There were six general areas on the DC-8 that furnished evidence of a collision:

1. Left wing leading edge. This is the forward portion of the airfoil of a wing (missing).
2. Left landing gear door. The door that protects the wheels when they're in a upright position (missing).
3. Right landing gear. The four wheels mounted on a strut (missing).
4. Number four engine. The DC-8 has four engines; numbers one and two are mounted on the left wing and numbers three and four are mounted on the right wing (missing).
5. Right wing outboard bend, ten degrees. (The outboard is the tip of the wing.)
6. The belly antenna. The antenna is placed on the belly of the plane for a better scan and reception (missing).

These parts were found among the TWA wreckage in Staten Island, New York; the rest of the jet crashed in Brooklyn. The aft section of the passenger cabin bounced off a brownstone and broke in two, coming to rest in a northerly direction on Sterling Place. The impact and subsequent fire aboard consumed most of the structure where the passengers were. The heat of the flames was such that identification of bodies was impossible. Upon impact, the right wing and number three engine, which were still attached, sliced through the Pillar of Fire Church. The flight deck with its three occupants came to rest in the same area and was largely consumed by fire. The left wing, except for the outer fifteen feet, came to rest in the intersection of the two streets with the outermost end aligned in a southwesterly direction. The fifteen-foot section of the wing that had broken off came to rest in a building at 126 Sterling Place, with two feet of the wing tip protruding through the building's roof. The empennage (tail assembly) and aft fuselage were found at Sterling Place on the south side of Seventh Avenue, facing north. Soot and blistered paint on the empennage provided evidence of fire onboard. The upper twenty-four inches of the paint-blistered rudder was damaged on ground impact, when it hit a truck at the south corner of the Sterling Place and Seventh Avenue intersection; the paint on the truck was exposed to the same ground fire heat. The left landing gear was found several feet from the Pillar of Fire Church. Bodies were found scattered along the streets of Sterling Place, on top of a truck, even dangling from the top of a lamp post. The rest were entombed in the wreckage.

Wreckage of United Flight 826, Seventh Ave. & Sterling Place
Park Slope Section of Brooklyn, December 16th 1960

Brooklyn
Flatbush Avenue
10:33:39 a.m.

The buildings of Brooklyn reminded me of the Lower East Side, and Flatbush Avenue reminded me of Delancey Street. Heading toward the bike shop, I felt the splattering of wet snow hitting the top of my head. It was strange, walking the streets of Brooklyn for the first time. Flatbush Avenue was a commercial avenue, filled with merchants all wanting to sell their products in time for the Christmas holiday. The streets and gutters were full of snow left there from the previous day; like Manhattan, everything was slushy and dirty. Reaching the other side of Flatbush, I took note of where the train station was for my return trip. With instructions in hand, I made my way through the busy crowd, hoping I was on the right street, and hoping that Joaquin gave me the right directions. As I walked, I thought of my friend Joaquin and wondered what he was doing. Was he getting better? I had been trying to reach his mother to see if I could go visit him, but I had not seen his family since he had been institutionalized; they seemed to have gone into seclusion, especially with the holidays around the corner. Walking toward Fourth Avenue, I found the streets unnaturally quiet. By now my shoes, which were supposed to keep my feet warm, were filled with slush. I didn't know where I was; I wanted to ask someone, but I was afraid they would ask why I wasn't in school.

According to Joaquin, all I had to do was cross Flatbush Avenue and walk two blocks. It seemed that I had been walking more than that as the train station got farther and farther away from my sight. I kept looking for a clock to see what time it was; I needed to know so that I could get back in time as my parents were waiting for me to help them in the store. I was going to give myself another hour, and if I didn't find it by then, I would head back to Manhattan without seeing my bike. Brightening up, I admitted to myself that I was, at least, having a pretty good time. So what if I didn't see my bike? I could always say that I traveled to Brooklyn on my own and back this was fun. And, of course, my parents would never know. Was this great or what? I went into a candy store and bought myself a candy bar, and took my time to get a little warm. I was drenched from the hailing rain, my coat was dripping, and my head was soaked. As I stepped out of the ice cream parlor, I decided to cross the street to check out some toy stores that were there. Standing outside looking in, I could see all kinds of toys lying around, some in boxes, others on the store floor, to show customers how they worked. I looked in store after store, but still saw no Schwinn bikes. I began to wonder if Joaquin had made a mistake. Could I be in the wrong neighborhood? Could it be that Joaquin, suffering from depression, gave me the wrong stop, or for that matter, the wrong borough? It was still early and I had plenty of time to look around. I dawdled in the store, chewing my candy, suddenly out of the corner of my eye I caught a glimpse of something, a sort of flash on top of a building, moving very fast. I thought nothing of it, and continued to eat my candy when all of a sudden a horrendous boom!

Seventh Ave. & Sterling Place.
December 16th 1960

Seventh Ave. and Sterling Place
Brooklyn
Friday, December 16
10:41 a.m.

They say that the road to hell is visible through the lens of one's eyes. They also say that if you've walked through it, you could exit a better person, regardless of age. It can also leave you helpless to forever go back to a natural and healthy life. If this is true, then I think I've just arrived. The scene looked like a set right out of a Hollywood movie, except it wasn't. It was very real. Standing there, my mind raced back to a couple of weeks ago, when our history teacher, Mr. Austin, taught us about World War II, showing us black-and-white stills of Europe, each frame showing pictures of ravaged cities, a reminder of man's destructive nature and how human life was wasted without guilt or remorse. The film showed graphic scenes, some of them made me uneasy sitting in my seat. I never was big on war; to me war was about two individuals who refuse to see the truth, who are unable to compromise with each other, who foster mass destruction. We saw file footage of bodies laying in the streets of Germany as buildings burned. The scene before my eyes in Brooklyn that day reminded me of such a place. It was bad, real bad, and for whatever reason I was a witness to it. And as much as I wanted to run away in apprehension and fear, I was too intrigued not to. I never knew what the term shock meant until that day, as I stood there in bewilderment and dismay, too young to understand what my eyes were confronting, too old to ever, ever forget it.

Within minutes, pandemonium set in as the people of Sterling Place were overcome with fear. As I stood there staring at the destruction before me, I thought of the little stupid things that Joaquin and I did as young

boys. Despite his illness, Joaquin was much braver than I was, and I thought
he would have been able to handle this. I wasn't sure I could. There was
hysteria everywhere. The row of buildings that moments before were aglow
with Christmas decorations had been invaded by death and chaos. Within
seconds of impact, their homes were in flames. The tenants came running
out dazed, numb, and frightened, and started running away from the scene
in confusion, running from the intense heat created by the ball of fire
that was the doomed jet. Many people were screaming for help, some in
their native language. People thought a bomb had hit Sterling Place. The
destruction was vast and extensive; everything was in ruins. The thick black
cloud following the three rapid explosions started to clear, and suddenly all
eyes were centered on a huge piece of metal in the middle of the street. It
was not a bomb, it was part of the tail and wing of a big plane.

The crew had tried desperately to make it to Prospect Park, but the
plane pancaked off the top of several six-story brownstones, leaving a path
of destruction, extending to several blocks. A jet engine was embedded in
front of one building, wiping out the entire face from the structure. I could
see tenants still in their nightwear inside the apartments. After cartwheeling
off the brownstones, the huge jet ballooned fifty feet into the air, blowing
up into several parts, coughing bodies out onto the icy streets below. The
jet plane self-destructed as it crashed into the Pillar of Fire Church. The
church, with its ninety-year-old caretaker inside, was demolished; of the
plane, only the tail section remained partially intact and you could partly
read The Mainliner DC-8 and big letters spelling United. It was United
Flight 826 out of Chicago.

The thick black smoke following the impact made it impossible to
see. My eyes were starting to itch as I made my way toward the wreckage.
The jet had dumped thousands of pounds of fuel, showering everything in
its path and making it difficult to breathe. There were bodies everywhere,
mostly mutilated. It terrified me. Within minutes, the place looked like a
war zone. All you could hear was a loud hum coming from the huge crowd,
all screaming in harmony, as terror gripped their souls. Looking down the
street, I could see rows of cars, all demolished and engulfed in flames. One
of the wings of the jet laid atop a truck. It had hit with such force that it
sliced the truck in two. The driver was nowhere to be found. In the middle
of the street was a dead man still strapped into his seat, laying sideways;
his face showed the fear he felt moments before his death. The street was
covered with bodies, too many to count; most were mutilated from the
impact, and the freezing rain slowly crept into their skin, a thin layer of ice

covering their bodies. I saw a body across the street. I had never seen death before, and, curious, I walked over to the body. It was a woman, wrapped around a fire hydrant. She hit the hydrant with such force that it was torn from its foundation. There was a puddle of blood in the snow, dripping from the side of her mouth. Her blue eyes were open, her long blonde hair soaked from the rain. The navy blue dress that she wore was partly burned, her hands, which moments before was neatly manicured, were now stained with her own blood.

The streets were littered with luggage that had been hurled from the plane when it blew up; some items had opened on impact. I noticed that the water from the rain, rushing toward the sewer, dragged with it the belongings of those who no longer would need any of it—toothbrushes, letters, and money. The water was tainted red with blood. Seeing it reminded me of what a neighbor once said about the revolution in Cuba, her home. There a rebel leader, young and strong, had gained the trust of many men and he intended to take control of the island. The overthrow would be a bloody one, and she said, "Tonight, blood will run down the streets of my beloved Cuba." I didn't know what she meant then, but I do now.

A Chinese man came running out of his laundry store, his body covered in flames. I'll never forget the agony in his face as he screamed for me to help him. I didn't know what to do but somehow I got the courage to throw him onto a puddle of water and tried to roll him around. But the fuel from the jet had penetrated his clothes and the water was of no use; it was like acid touching your skin. I left him there still screaming, as I continued my way toward the wreckage. A young man ran into me, knocking me to the ground. He was holding his left arm and his face was covered in blood. He mindlessly ran in circles, screaming they're all dead! He was one of the witnesses of the actual crash, and saw the bodies as they burned beyond recognition. I can still see him after all these years. I felt lost and unbalanced, as everything around me went by in slow motion.

Unknown to any of us, in New Dorp, Staten Island, ten miles away, a second plane had come down. George Dorfman, a real estate broker, driving along Staten Island's Hylan Boulevard, heard a terrible grinding sound that made him think something had gone wrong with his car. He shut off his engine, stepped out, and realized that the noise was coming from a plane about three hundred feet overhead. He watched in horror as the burning plane broke up into several parts and showered debris over a wide area. It was TWA Flight 266, inbound to LaGuardia; its wreckage had narrowly missed a neighborhood of houses and a public school. Witnesses said that the bodies in the blood-drenched snow made them think of a battlefield. Most of the Staten Island observers of the falling TWA plane mentioned the sickening horror of watching the slow earthward spiraling of the fuselage that carried so many to their death. Clifford Beuth, an oil delivery man who later testified at a hearing, said that he saw the plane come down in three parts, he went on to state that the front part of the plane, missing an engine, was spiraling toward earth.

Then I saw an engine on the right side blow up. The second engine also on the right side blew after that, and when it did, it blew the tail section into pieces. I watched in horror as people were falling out of the plane, and said out loud, "Oh God."

Another witness who testified was Frank Maybury, a Staten Island dispatcher for the Transit Authority buses. Maybury was in the company's car at New Dorp Lane and Hylan Boulevard when he heard a noise like a jet breaking the sound barrier. He said he looked up in disbelief as the burning fuselage blew up, sending parts of bodies falling to earth. He picked up a policeman who was on foot patrol and headed for Miller Field, while notifying police by radio to get fire and other equipment rolling. Maybury and the policeman picked up parts of bodies that had fallen along Hylan Boulevard and gathered them on Miller Field, where, he later said, "The snow was red with blood."

One of the most dramatic testimonies was given by Norman Fowler, a Brooklyn resident and a truck driver for the Railway Express Trucking Company. For the past five years, his routine was the same. Every morning, he would get up, give thanks to the Lord for another day, kiss his wife, Gloria, and their children good-bye, pick up his truck, and head out to do his daily deliveries. His first stop was the coffee shop at the corner of Seventh Avenue and Sterling Place, and he was well known there because it was one of his stops throughout the day. That morning, like every other morning, Norman had stopped to get his coffee and buttered roll. The snow was rapidly turning into wet ice, making it difficult for him to park his truck at his usual spot, so he settled for a spot a few yards down the street in Sterling Place. Walking to the coffee shop, he heard a strange sound but didn't think anything of it; strange sounds were common in the early morning hours, especially on weekdays. He figured it was a muffler backfiring. Approaching the door to the restaurant, he heard the sound getting louder and closer as though it were right above him. He looked up and was astounded by what he saw: a jet plane out of control. He watched in horror as the plane sideswiped a building, causing an engine to fly off the wing. His heart beat uncontrollably as his eyes followed the path of the 4,000-pound engine, which crashed onto his truck, demolishing it completely. A cold sweat swept his entire body as the reality of what had just happened hit him, sending a chilling sensation up his spine. He said he heard a faint humming sound coming from one of the engines; it seemed like it was the only one working.

"I could see that he, the pilot, was in trouble, Fowler testified. He must have been trying to land the crippled jet at Prospect Park, where there was plenty of open space, because for a minute it seemed he picked up a little altitude, but then he lost power on the only working engine. I watched as the plane just glided; there was no sound. The plane clipped the side of a building with its left wing, hitting the row of houses."

Fowler went on to say that there was an explosion as the plane crashed into a church just a few feet from where the coffee shop stood. Within minutes, the peaceful morning had turned into chaos, bodies everywhere. He said he helped firemen with their hoses until "the cops chased me away."

The streets of Seventh Ave. were packed with onlookers. People raced around in circles not knowing where they were headed. Others, like me, just stood in disbelief. Traffic was at a standstill; you could hear sirens, but it was difficult for help to get through. The freezing rain continued relentlessly. I remember that my shoes were soaked and all I kept thinking of was home, and how I wished I was there. I stood staring in amazement at this huge piece of metal which towered over me approximately ten feet away. I could feel the heat from it. Three bodies lay on top of each other, tangled in the rubbish. A thin layer of smoke wafted up into the cold air, dissipating immediately. A black purse, partially open, half-burned, lay on the ground. Out of the corner of my eye, I saw an arm move. Thinking this person was still alive, I raced over to them, my heart pounding. I could see the white shirt drench in blood, a man's shirt. When I got there, I stared in horror to see that it was only an arm, torn off at the shoulder, a wedding band still on the finger. I ran away in panic, slipping on the ice and falling in the middle of the street. A woman helped me get to my feet; she said something in a foreign language and smiled, a strange smile of fear, and then continued running away.

I have often wondered why I stayed. I should have taken the train back to Manhattan, but I didn't. As I tried to compose myself from the fall, I kept thinking why was this happening. Was it an act from God? I walked over and sat down on the stoop of a burned building, demolished by the crash. I was too tired and numb to do anything. As I stared at the destruction left by the plane, I took in the full impact of what had happened. I tried to think what I could do to make a difference, but nothing came to mind.

The sirens were getting louder, indicating that help was not far away. By then, the crowd had settled down, as they started their own search-and-rescue operation. I looked as far as my tired eyes could see and all I saw was destruction—buildings, cars, all destroyed. Smoke was everywhere as flames engulfed the entire community; buildings burned to the ground, firefighters unable to rescue them.

My ambition to learn how to fly went out of my mind on that day. I didn't want to die this way. All I felt was tremendous pain for all those who had perished.

Paul Geidel and Rescue Company One
Midtown Fire Company
10:45 a.m.

Traffic was at a crawl as the Mack truck with siren blasting made its way toward downtown Manhattan, heading toward the Manhattan Bridge to Brooklyn. The bells, ten of them, had rung minutes before in the firehouse, and the entire crew of firefighters scrambled onto the freezing streets of New York. Inside the fire truck, Lieutenant Michael Gerus was monitoring the mobile radio, trying to find out what type of situation they were going to. Bill Reilly, the driver of the small but powerful truck, was having a hard time managing the truck in the weather and it swerved from side to side. Ten alarms meant that something catastrophic had happened, but for reasons unknown the communication radio of Rescue One was inoperable. By now, news of the crash had hit the airwaves and everyone from New York to Washington knew of the crash except Rescue One. In the back of the cramped Mack, the men were gearing up, still wondering what they were going to.

William McMahon, Paul Geidel's closest friend, was trying to get his right boot on while maintaining his balance in the moving fire truck. Looking at Paul with a half grin, William said, "Well, Pauley, I guess going home early is a thing of the past."

"What do you mean?"

"Something bad has happened in Brooklyn, something really bad. We're going to be there all night."

"Hey, boss, any word on what we're getting into?" asked Paul.

"No word yet, men. Just keep gearing up, this might be nasty."

"It's probably another building that caught fire due to a Christmas tree," said Ronald McGhee.

Paul Geidel
F.D.N.Y. Rescue One

"Come on, McGhee," said Paul. "Do you really think a burning building is a ten-alarm?"

"Okay," answered Ron, with a grin in his face. "So two buildings are burning."

The two men in the front were getting frustrated. The Lieutenant Gerus was still trying to communicate with someone in Brooklyn, but was unsuccessful. Bill Reilly was trying to negotiate the traffic, but the slush and freezing rain kept cars and trucks from pulling over to the side. The men were now stuck in the middle of the Manhattan Bridge. Annoyed, Bill rolled down the window and shouted at motorists to get out of the way. Looking out the little windows of the truck Paul suddenly shouted, "Hey guys, look at that! It looks like the whole block is burning. Hey, McGhee, looks more like 20 buildings are burning."

"Holy shit," said McGhee. "Would you look at that? The whole fucking place is in smoke."

Approaching the end of the bridge, a police officer emerged from inside a police cruiser and waved frantically at the men of Rescue One. He ran toward the Mack truck as Lieutenant Gerus opened the window and leaned out to hear what the officer, who was out of breath, had to say,

"Lieutenant, you can't go through there. It's too congested and you'll never make it in time."

"In time for what?"

"Just follow me, sir. Please, let's hurry. There's no time to lose."

Miller Airfield
Staten Island, NY
10:46 a.m.

Debris from the TWA wreckage was scattered all over the wet and mushy field. The impact from the plane had made a huge crater, and parts of the plane still burned. The heat was unapproachable. By now, the little community of Staten Island knew of the collision. Rescue units had arrived at the scene, but it was too late; all that was left of the Constellation was rubble. The flight deck had separated from the fuselage, its captain and two officers still inside, presumed dead. One of its engines was emitting a thin layer of smoke, as the black oil remaining in the oil lines burned. The fuselage, still containing passengers, burned uncontrollably.

A huge part of another plane, what seemed to be a jet engine, was partially buried in the ground. It belonged to the United jet that had crashed ten miles away. Bodies had been hurled out into the field; some were covered with mud, unrecognizable from a distance. Human parts blanketed Hylan Boulevard two miles away. Motorists on the boulevard at first thought that the flesh they saw was from some form of dead animal struck by a car or truck. It soon became obvious that something else had happened. A badly burned torso was found by a young man walking his dog. A milkman, on his way back to the company after finishing his early morning delivery, crashed into a fence to avoid hitting what he later said was a lacerated leg from the hip down, laying in the middle of the road, his shoe still on.

A body hung from a tree along Hylan Boulevard, dangling as the wind fluttered it from side to side. A young mother carrying an infant in her arms walked in a daze along the street; she had fled in fear when the rear half of the fuselage landed just three hundred feet from her home. She would later

Wreckage of Twa 266. Staten Island, New York
December 16th 1960

tell authorities that the silver object had split open in half like a seashell, some bodies still inside.

A few miles down, two off-duty policemen who were brothers were shopping in a toy store, when they heard the sound from Miller Airfield, not far from them. They knew by the sound that something terrible had happened. Leaving their presents in the store, the brothers raced down the street and climbed the wire fence that surrounded the airfield. They would later testify in a public hearing that they were the first to arrive at the scene. One brother tried to cut the strapped passengers from the burning wreckage with his knife. Both said all was silent inside.

Colonel E. M. Huwan, the commander of the military station, said that while lives were lost in this tragic event, God had brought the plane in. When asked what he meant, he said that pieces of the ill-fated plane had landed in the backyard of a nearby school, P.S. 41, just two blocks away, and that another school, P.S. 11, had an entire engine fall just steps from the yard where kids played. Fortunately, the weather had kept the children inside.

Although twisted and burned shards rained down on Hylan Boulevard, no one on the ground was injured. At the Miller Field staff members supplied green blankets from their barracks to cover the bodies, laying them in rows on the blood-stained snow.

A Red Cross helicopter with bright red lettering landed at the field to airlift two passengers to a nearby hospital; both died en route. In Washington, go team one from the Civil Aeronautics Board was gearing up, getting ready to travel to New York. This was now the worst air disaster they had encountered, surpassing the crash of 1956 when two plane collided over the Grand Canyon in Arizona, killing 128 aboard both planes. Ironically, the same companies were involved today.

The Mallory Family
Broad Street
Summit, New Jersey
10:46:45 a.m.

By now live reports of the tragic event were on every radio and television station; some were reporting from the crash site in Staten Island, some from Sterling Place in Brooklyn. The Mallory's home, which earlier had been full of happiness and joy, was now full of horror and dismay as Annie Lou, William, and their son William Jr. stared at the television, not believing what they were seeing or hearing. The news media spoke of the midair collision of two planes, but they were having trouble confirming the flight numbers.

Annie finally ran weeping to her room, not wanting to hear the explicit details of the scene. She lay curled up on her bed, squeezing her pillow for comfort. In the living room a broken-hearted father sat with his head bowed, while his eldest son tried to convince them both that it was not Darnell's plane that had crashed.

"Dad," said William, "it could be another plane. There're lots of United planes. We don't know for sure if it was Darnell's."

"Call your sister. Tell her to call the airlines. Tell her to find out. Better yet, tell her to go to the airport instead. Go ahead, Junior, call. I'm gonna go to check on your mother."

William Jr. went to get his sister's phone number when the phone rang. It was Shirley Dean. She was hysterical, sobbing uncontrollably, and it was hard for William to understand her. Slow down, Shirley he said.

"Billy, is it Darnell's plane? Is it?"

"I'm trying to find out, Shirley. I have to call Mordine."

"Call me back, Billy. Promise me you'll call me back."

"I promise, Shirley Dean, I promise. Let me call my sister first. Oh shit, I forgot I have to pick up Johnny. I don't want him to be alone if word gets out in school. I'll call you back."

A knock on the door broke the tension that the young William was feeling. Hanging up the phone, he ran to the door. It was Ralph, a close friend of Darnell. He had heard the news and ran over to be with his friend's family. His thin body was shaking from the grief that he felt inside.

"Billy, is it true? Is it Darnell's plane?"

"I'm trying to call my sister in New York to find out."

"Where's your mom and dad?"

"Inside. Mom's not doing too well."

Just then the phone rang; it was Mordine. Being the eldest she tried to control her emotions but failed. Weeping, she said she had already called the airport and their worst fears were realized. United had confirmed Flight 826 from Chicago was the plane that had crashed in Brooklyn.

"Billy, tell mom and dad that Darnell was one of the passengers in that plane."

"Come home, sis, right away. I don't know how I'm going to tell them. Come home now. Please."

"Billy, be strong. I have to go to the airport. Call Shirley, tell her to come over to help you with mom and dad."

"Shirley called already. She's hysterical, Mordine. Please come home now."

"Okay, Billy, I'm on my way. Don't tell them anything until I get there."

Hanging up Billy bowed his head and began to cry and Ralph rushed to his side to comfort him. For them the waiting was over, and just begun was the grief. Unable to control himself, Bill ask Ralph to get Johnny at school. Ralph zippered his jacket and with tears in his eyes headed out the door. As he walked down the street he remembered seven months earlier, when he and Darnell were celebrating their graduation from Summit High, and how Darnell had laughed, marveling at his acceptance to the University of Omaha. Ralph could still see him dancing with Shirley Dean and his big smile, a smile of life, accomplishment, and happiness.

He stopped to stare at the building in front of him, their high school. Ralph walked inside, realizing with immense sadness that the next time he saw his friend it would be to say good-bye.

Sixth Avenue & Sterling Place
Brooklyn
11:01 a.m.

Never have I seen so many people gathered in one place at one time. Mainly people were scrambling to safety, making the whole scene frightening. Hearing the sound of sirens, I pushed myself toward the sound. I could see the heavy traffic caused by the crash and the red fire truck, Engine Company 269 from nearby, stuck in the middle of it. Foot patrolmen from the area were trying in vain to divert trucks and cars. The sound of wheels could be heard spinning, unable to move forward.

The first alarm was issued at 10:41 a.m. It had been half an hour since the plane had tumbled out of the sky. The fire truck was long and had a ladder lying across the top. It also had two drivers, one in the front and one in the back. Steering the huge truck was a difficult; both drivers were maneuvering to avoid hitting the parked cars.

Why don't you just get off the truck and run to the scene? I thought to myself, when suddenly they did just that. Standing in the corner with the rain and wind hitting my face, I saw these young men running toward the crash site, their axes in hand and oxygen tanks strapped to their backs. Following them were police officers dressed in black rain coats and black hats, their silver badges visible. Their uniforms were drenched.

I turned my attention to the middle of the block, where the big chuck of debris still smoldered. Then I saw something even more disturbing, if that was possible, than the destruction surrounding me, something so inconceivable it is hard to put into words. To my right were the brave men racing toward the crash site, toward me; to my left was the destruction, a nightmare difficult to grasp. But now looters had descended into the area, vultures who had no respect for human life or the victims who lay beneath the rubble. I was flooded with anger but too scared to say anything, caught between beauty and horror. My attention shifted back to the racing battalions of firefighters, who at last were almost to the scene. I turned to the ugliness again, watching with disgust as certain individuals pried into the pockets of some of the victims who were but minutes dead. I could see them searching through the luggage, feeding their pockets with belongings, and running away while they laughed like hyenas. It was appalling. By now, the first wave of firemen's was turning the corner, approaching the crash site. The wind was ripping into my body, and the tingling sensation from the freezing rain numbed my face. I struggled to keep my eyes open. Suddenly, there he was, the first fireman from Engine 269 to arrive in front of me. I tried to move out of his way but wasn't fast enough. The fireman, easily double my weight, unintentionally ran into me and knocked me down. He turned and looked back as he ran, making sure I wasn't injured. I sat on the wet concrete, my back to the building, as the rest of the men ran by. They were shouting something to each other, focusing on the tail section of the plane; all were amazed by what they saw, at what they were about to face.

Getting up again, I wiped my pants, which were soaked and starting to ice up. I started to run back into the crowed street, when another, smaller, fire truck arrived, preceded by a police car that paved their way. I watched as the small truck made its way in. It was red and had gold block-type lettering that read Rescue Unit One. Unlike the fire trucks that I have seen, this one didn't have the men riding on the back and sides. In fact, it appeared to be empty. The small Mack truck stopped a few yards from the entrance into the street, as the heavy litter that had spread across a couple of blocks didn't allow them to get closer. I waited to see what this little red truck was going to do; where were the firemen? Suddenly, like in the movies, the door to the back of the truck opened and inside were the men from Rescue One. They came out one by one, seeming to me to be moving in slow motion. I don't know how many came out of the little truck, but they looked so cool, as they ran in formation into the place I had coined shattered dreams. It seemed that hours had past since history was made in this little part of New York, but it had been minutes. Suddenly, without warning, a loud explosion was heard on the other side of Sterling Place by Seventh Avenue.

The crowd again ran in fear. I couldn't see what had just occurred, but I saw a small black object hurl through the air, reaching over the top of the four-story brownstones, now destroyed. Then it made a 180-degree turn and headed toward the frightened people below. I don't know where it landed.

Strangely, mixed with all the chemicals and toxic that burned there that day chemicals that probably contributed to the death of many passengers while still airborne was the smell of pine. I don't know where it came from, but it was calming, a relief from the odor of spilled fuel, burning rubber, and burning flesh.

Time had stopped for me: the bike that I had come here was forgotten, as was the grocery store on Avenue C in Manhattan, where I had to be by noon. Nothing mattered anymore but what was before me. I had passed the test, walked into the valley of the dead. And dreadful as it was, I didn't want to leave. The test was in my heart and my empty stomach. I was captivated by the burning buildings, the smoldering cars, the giant tail, the looters, the screaming, and the bodies. I couldn't let go; I couldn't climb back onto the train. I had to see this through.

Hemet, California
The Sawyers' residence
8:10 a.m., PST

It was impossible to get through to United Airlines, though Patricia Sawyers phoned again and again and again. Unable to focus properly, she was in a state of shock and ran from room to room, unable to quiet her pounding heart. She turned on the television in the living room and the radio in her bedroom. She wanted to hear the news but she wanted the truth to go away. She first heard the news on her car radio, just after she had dropped her three daughters off at school.

The last thing she remembered was Robert telling her was that he was going to New York. She repeated it to herself over and over in a struggle to reject the inevitable. He went straight from here to New York. The plane that crashed was from Chicago.

A knock on the door broke the suspense. She walked toward the door in fear, not knowing who was on the other side. Getting closer to the door, something told her to run. Suddenly, a sense of apprehension froze her movements. Her body went numb and she stumbled just inches from the door, unable to reach the door knob. She dragged herself along the wall of the living room, perspiring. Feeling helpless, she started to sob, then to scream, a scream of fear and pain. She knew that a representative of her husband's company might be on the other side of the door. She didn't want to hear or welcome them. Finally, gathering all her strength, Patricia stood up, wiped the tears from her face, took a deep breath, and opened the door.

Rescue Unit One
Sterling Place
11:33 a.m.

The men from Rescue One, like soldiers, stood still waiting for their instructions from their commanding officer, Lieutenant Gerus. As they stood in the cold, their trained eyes swept the entire area. All focused on the big chunk of metal in the middle of the street, which towered over each object in the area. The men from Engine Company 169 were already busy fighting fires in several local stores that were engulfed in flames. Others were foaming the burning cars. The howling wind and freezing rain made it difficult for the platoon to hear their lieutenant's commands.

Listen up, men. Paul, you, and William Reilly are team one. I want you to head up to the top of that building over there and start assisting the men from Engine 169. Ron, you, and Bill Curran will be team two. Head toward the tail of the plane. Stay alert. I don't want any injuries on my shift. The rest of you, McMahon and Joe Reres, you're team three, follow me.

The building that the lieutenant was talking about was adjacent to the Pillar of Fire Church, which was in flames. Part of the roof had been destroyed by one of the plane's engines; the stairs were unstable as panic-stricken tenants tried in vain to get out by running down the stairs. The hallway of each floor was partially destroyed, partially aflame. Dragging the hose up the stairs, the main concern of Bill and Paul was the building's structure, whether it was safe. Their troubles were just beginning, though, as frightened tenants, most still in their pajamas, some carrying infants, and all frantic to get out of the building, made it almost impossible for the firefighters to continue up the stairs. The heat was intense, so intense that some of the occupants from the second floor had minor burns on their faces and arms from the fire that raged at the top of the building. Reaching the top, the firemen continued

F.D.N.Y.
Rescue One
From Left, William Curran, Paul Geidel,
Ronald Mcghee, William Reilly

to the section where they had been ordered. Opening the door to the roof, the men were stunned by what they saw.

Down below, it was mayhem; policemen were attempting to restore order as they tried to seal the area off to onlookers. The bodies of all the victims remained where they had died; it would be a long time before doctors from the coroner's office would arrive. By now, food was no longer an issue in my mind and I was no longer bothered by the cold as I walked over the bodies. The priests from the nearby church were kneeling down over victims, performing last rites, their faces full of emotion.

At first, I didn't take too much notice on the extent of the casualties. Down the street, volunteers from the Red Cross, among them nurses wearing navy blue coats, were embarking from their van. They immediately started to administer to hundreds of people on the streets who had been injured by debris from the crash. The police department had taken a theater as a shelter for those whose homes had been destroyed. A Texaco garage was also taken over to place the corpses from the streets and sidewalks. One body was sprawled over a burning car; he just lay there, embedded on the hood of this green car, its paint slowly fading from the heat of the fire. Another car sat in the middle of the street, its engine still running; inside the crushed car was a woman, her hands still on the steering wheel and blood dripping slowly from her left ear, her nostrils trickling drops of blood onto her dress. As I circle the car, looking in the back of the seat, I could see that she had just come from buying groceries; the two grocery bags had torn from the impact and I could see baby formula was among the items. Part of a wing was wrapped alongside the car.

As I stood there looking at the woman in the crushed car, another event was unfolding on the roof where firefighters Paul Geidel and William Reilly were.

"Holy Shit," yelled Bill. "There are bodies up here. Paul, call for medical backup."

"Bill, they're dead."

"How the hell would you know? Make the call!"

"I'll make the call, Bill, but do you think they're alive, lying there like that? Just look at them, man, look at them. Our concern now is to put out the fire, so let's do it. Give me more hose, let's get this fire out, and get the hell out of here. This building is about to collapse and I don't want to be around when it does."

Their conversation was interrupted when Lieutenant Gerus came on the CB radio, asking their position and the condition of the roof. Looking up in their direction as he talked to them, Gerus could see a massive fragment of bricks had ripped away when the jet's wing and turbine had made contact. He also noticed that at the corner of the demolished building part of the wall was starting to crumble, falling into the Pillar of Fire Church. His heart suddenly ached when he realized that at any moment the four-story building might collapse with his men on top of it. He reminded himself that he had promised all his men that they would go home to their families unharmed.

"Rescue One leader to team one, come in, over."

"Yeah, go ahead, leader, this is Paul, over."

"Paul, what's the scoop up there? over."

"Lieutenant, the place is a mess. There's basically no roof left, the building has been evacuated, and there's part of the plane up here. Team leader, there're also two, I repeat two bodies up here. At this time, we can't confirm whether they are passengers or tenants. Please advise, over."

"Listen, Paul, you need to secure the area and get out. By the look from down here it is not too good. I'm having Bill turn on the hose. Stand by, over and out."

The men walked toward the edge of the building, getting ready for the water to come alive. As they reached the edge, they saw the ruins of the church next door where the plane had made its resting place. Leaning over almost at the tip, Paul and Bill took in the view from above, disturbed to see parts of bodies entrenched in the wreckage.

Suddenly, Paul felt a jolt. It was coming from the hose as water raced from below. The men held the hose firmly, preparing for the wicked power of the water in the hose. The snow and debris on the roof made it difficult for the men of Rescue One to stand without losing their balance, and the pressure from the hose would put both men to the test. Suddenly, a clamp from the hose busted, sending a gush of freezing water through the seams of the hose, splattering the two men with force and leaving them drenched from head to toe. Parts of the roof began to sway from side to side as the men holding the hose tried to replace the defective clamp. A crumbling sound took their attention as part of the roof gave way. The sound of crashing debris was felt on the streets as screams were heard. The men could see the apartments of the fourth floor just below them.

"This is no good, Bill. We have to get out of here. Team leader, this is team one. We are abandoning premises. The roof is gone, permission to evacuate over."

"Get the hell out of there, Paul. Evacuate. I repeat, evacuate."

Idlewild Airport
Queens, New York
United Terminal
11:21 a.m.

Agonizing suspense and grief filled the United Airlines waiting room at Idlewild after relatives and friends of the passengers aboard United Flight 826 learned the plane had crashed in Brooklyn. The crowd knew something was wrong when the flight was removed from the illuminated board, but confirmation of the disaster was withheld for at least an hour. When airline officials finally revealed that there had been an accident and when it became increasingly clear that there were many dead among the seventy-seven passengers and seven crew members aboard, many men and women in the lounge began to weep. In the corner of the lounge, a woman sobbed quietly to herself; she was waiting for her husband, whom she married less than a month earlier.

"What am I going to do, what am I going to do?" she said, as tears ran down her cheek.

Strangers that didn't know her came to her side, assuring her that maybe her husband was still alive.

"No, no," she sobbed. "The radio said there was only one survivor. It's not him. He's dead."

"Maybe he missed the flight," suggested a woman.

"No, he called me from the airport to say good morning to me."

Attention shifted as the door of the private lounge suddenly opened. A visibly shaken airline representative emerged, accompanied by a local priest. The presence of the priest confirmed everyone's fears as strangers, friends, and family members hugged one another in grief. Except for the sobbing among the stricken ones, the lounge was almost completely silent. The sound of the Christmas carols could be heard over the public speakers.

A moment of silence was observed as the priest said a prayer for those who had perished and those who might have survived. Then the representative, her voice quivering, made the announcement. "On behalf of this airline, I want to express my condolences to each and every one of you. I can only imagine what you're going through right now. A little less than an hour ago, we got confirmation that a United DC-8 out of Chicago inbound to this airport, crashed in Brooklyn. Despite what the news media is reporting, the truth is that it's too early to say what happened. What we do know is that United Flight 826 out of Chicago, and due to land at Idlewild at approximately 10:41 a.m., crashed in Brooklyn a little less than an hour ago. We are providing you with transportation to Kings County Hospital in Brooklyn, where they are bringing all those involved. What I want you to do right now is to get all your belongings and follow me please."

Among those were Mordine Mallory, Phyllis Baltz, and Phyllis's daughter, Randee.

Twelve miles away at LaGuardia Airport, the same scene was being played, as worried family members and friends were left stunned by reports of a crash on Staten Island. Most of the people who had been waiting for the doomed plane left immediately upon hearing of the crash, deciding to travel in their own cars to the Bellevue Hospital morgue in Manhattan to identify their loved ones. Some stayed behind, hoping that someone would tell them that their loved ones had missed the flight due to weather. An elderly couple, whose son and daughter-in-law were bringing their fourteen-day-old granddaughter, stopped a representative from the airline.

"My son, Peter Greibel, and his wife, Karen were coming from Ohio with our granddaughter. She was only fourteen days old. Please tell us they weren't aboard."

I can't answer that. I don't know. You should go to Manhattan. I'm so sorry.

They waited until their hopes were gone, then, like the others, headed to the morgue and the ordeal of searching among the bodies. Meanwhile, the rescue operations continued at both crash sites and in Washington, speculation as to what had happened began.

Jacob Riis Housing
The Lower East Side
12:30 p.m.

News of the accident had circulated quickly around the Lower East Side. The Spanish radio by now had broadcast the event and the Spanish Television Network was on its way to broadcast live from the crash site in Brooklyn.

On the snowy and gushy streets of the East Side, all conversation was about the accident. Many wondered whether either plane had come from Puerto Rico or Santo Domingo, in the Dominican Republic, since planes from both were also scheduled to land at Idlewild and LaGuardia. Inside my father's store, on the counter, an old beat-up radio was giving details about the crash as live coverage was now starting to come in. Local customers in the bodega were glued to the radio; for many, they were just learning of the accident. Meanwhile my father was busy counting the boxes that were being delivered by the Goya company. Looking out the front glass window, he noticed that the snow was coming down much heavier than before as the driver and his helper continued to unload the boxes from their double-parked tractor trailer. Leaving his trusted friends in the store, my father went out to finish counting the boxes, as the blistering wind swept through his grayish hair. He kept looking toward Seventh Street, where I usually made the turn when coming from school, and wondered where the hell I was.

My mother had already left. Weather had slowed business, so she had decided to go and prepare dinner for us. At home, she had the radio on as news of the deadly crash came pouring in, including reports of ground casualties. She was seasoning a chicken when she heard a knock at the door. Walking slowly while cleaning her hands on her apron, she turned the knob and opened the door. It was her neighbor from the second floor,

Anna, standing with her son Robert. Robert was one of my friends, and the only one who knew I was playing hooky that day; he also knew that I was going to Brooklyn. Giving him a nudge, Anna told Robert to repeat to my mother what he had told her.

Robert Cruz, or mousey, as Joaquin called him, was a skinny little kid with buck teeth and funny ears that stuck out, like those of a mouse. To tell Mousey to keep a secret was like telling the news media to keep quiet. By the time he got to school that day, everyone, including the teacher, knew where I was. He stood there crying as he told my mother where I was. My mother, feeling nauseous, calmly invited them in, walked to the phone, and called the store. Mr. Alma, a family friend, answered.

"Mr. Alma, is Raymond there?" (My mother never called me Ray.)

"No, Mrs. Garcia, he's not."

"Where is Tino?"

"He's here," said Mr. Alma, becoming concerned.

"Please put him on right away."

Mr. Alma whispered something into my father's ear. Walking back to the phone, my father asked Mr. Alma whether he knew what it was about.

I don't know, he replied, but she did mention Raymond. Somehow Dad knew beforehand that it was about me. "Maybe I had had to stay after school," he thought to himself, "or maybe he got sick." Picking up the phone, his wife of thirty years said, "Tino, Raymond didn't go to school today." She paused for a moment, then gave way to her emotions. Sobbing she said, "Raymond is at the crash site. He went looking for that stupid bike you promised him. Reports are that at least six people on the ground are confirmed dead, and one kid is reported in critical condition."

Hylan Boulevard
Staten Island, NY
1:45 p.m.

The sun, breaking through the grayish clouds, gleamed down on Hylan Boulevard as New York police officers went house-to-house, searching for bodies and wreckage from the plane, which had disintegrated in midair. Motorists were flooding the police department with reports of bodies alongside the roadway.

Fires from burning trees were also being reported, as scared tenants worried that their houses might catch fire. Units from the fire department in neighboring New Jersey were dispatched to help Staten Islanders battle the raging fires that had spread across a one-mile radius from the crash. The fuel from the Constellation plane was showering everything within its path, igniting fires below. Not far away, a paddy wagon followed policemen and volunteers from nearby who had joined in the search for survivors. Inside the wagon were a paramedic and a priest. At the crash site, the Army was preventing spectators, some who had arrived within minutes of the crash, from getting near.

By now, the sun had coated the entire East Coast and began to melt the snow, making the area in the field mushy and muddy.

In the wreckage, the grim task of searching for survivors was almost done, as parts of bodies were being laid on the pavement, leading to one of the airfield's runways. Most of the victims were unrecognizable, with burns so bad it was impossible even to discern their gender. At the outer fence, curious citizens, hands to their face and expressions of disbelief and horror, stared at the carnage.

An elderly woman, dressed only in a nightgown, ran down Hylan Boulevard, hands flailing and screaming. She ran toward the men who were marching down the middle of the street with bullhorns asking tenants to report any wreckage that might have fallen into their backyards.

"Help me, someone, help me," the distraught woman screamed.

Grabbing the sergeant by his collar, the heavyset woman, breathing heavily and her eyes bulging, kept screaming for someone to help. She was in total shock, she was quivering, she was also perspiring not from the cold but from what had fallen in her backyard. With a sudden twist, she headed back to the same way she had arrived, at the same time motioning with her right hand for the rescuers to follow her.

"Come, come," she cried out in Polish. "Hurry! Hurry! They might be alive!"

The team jumped to action as the twenty-four men raced down the street through the wet and slushy snow, gear in tow, trying to catch up to the woman, hoping that somehow a miracle had taken place. The woman, half a block ahead of them, made a right turn into her residential area and disappeared from view. Arriving at the intersection, they saw a small and frightened crowd gathered around a home, pointing toward the alley, leading to her yard.

"Come, come look over here," said the woman, emerging from the back with her hand at her chest, her face gripped with hysteria.

"Oh my god!" was all that came out of the sergeant as his team stood silent.

There in the back yard, embedded in the grass, part of the fuselage of the Connie, its red and white colors identifying the TWA. It was part of a side of the rear fuselage, approximately fourteen feet long, and there was an intact window. The men could see a man's head leaning against the window, his left hand sticking out of the fuselage as though he was trying to remove the debris that covered his bruised and wounded body.

Hemet, California
The Sawyers' residence
10:47 a.m., PST

A black sedan with a government plate stood parked outside the quiet suburb street where Captain Robert Sawyer resided. Inside were two men, dressed in black with crisp white shirts and neatly placed ties, standing by the grieving widow. Their task was to inform her of her husband's fate. One man was from the Civil Aeronautics Board, the other was a representative from United Airlines. Looking out the window, Patricia noticed a small crowd of her friends and neighbors had started to gather outside her home. The two men were there to answer any questions that Mrs. Sawyers might have, as well as to answer any questions from the media, who were expected to arrive at any time. Their main job, however, was to prevent Patricia from saying anything that might jeopardize the government's investigation into the cause of the crash. Looking around, one of the men noticed a picture of Robert Sawyer in his airline uniform, his smile expressing achievement and pride. The two men looked at each other, and then the United representative walked over to the window and grabbed the picture.

"What are you doing?" said Patricia. "Why are you taking Robert's picture down?"

"Ma'am, this is a precaution. The media is going to be here any minute and we don't want them to take a snapshot of your husband, not yet. They have already decided that your husband was at fault, so we're here to protect your family's privacy. That's how your husband would have wanted it."

Placing a chair next to sobbing woman, the young representative from the Civil Aeronautics Board took out a pen from his jacket and opened a loose-leaf notebook and sat down. He faced Patricia and took a minute to look at her. With concern, he said,

"Mrs. Sawyer, I can only imagine how you're feeling right now. I need to ask you some questions. Some might be a little personal. You don't have to answer them, but I must ask them. The reason we're here is to keep you from being dragged to a public hearing and to answer any questions you might have. Is that okay with you, Mrs. Sawyer?"

Leaning over, Patricia took the picture from the man's hand and held it close to her. Staring at the picture, she answered politely, "My daughters are in school."

"Okay, we're going to send a squad car to pick them up, all right?"

"Okay," she said.

The United man walked over to the phone, picked it up, and made the call. The man sitting looked at Patricia and assured her that everything was going to be all right. But he knew that it was only the beginning of what would become a grueling interview with a woman who had just lost her husband. A woman who six hours earlier had watched her husband kiss his sleeping daughters good-bye.

Just then the media arrived, knocking on the door. Confused and frightened, Patricia pressed the picture to her chest, trying to shield herself from the nightmare she was experiencing. Seeing her anguish, the Board member said, "Don't worry, Mrs. Sawyer, they won't come in. It's against the law, so don't worry."

"Shall we start with the questions?"

"Yes," she replied.

Back in Brooklyn, chaos still loomed in the air. It had been four hours since the crash and by now the fires that had destroyed most of the blocks had been extinguished or at least brought under control. There were so many curious onlookers and their numbers increased with every passing hour that the police were unable to keep them restrained within an isolated area. Most of the curious were from the surrounding neighborhood; most were there to help in the grim task that followed. With the fires almost all out, all eyes were focused on the Pillar of Fire Church, or what was left of it. Our attention was on the row of men, lined up against the building that hours before was engulfed in flames, the same building I saw two firemen enter before. The men leaning against the wall were team members from the Coast Guard, the Red Cross, and auxiliary medics, all dressed in black raincoats that glittered from the freezing rain. They were teamed up in twos, a folded stretcher between them. Their job was to transport the remains. I nicknamed them the wooden soldiers.

Inside, the rubble firemen searched for bodies, moving metal and bricks one piece at a time with their bare hands. The impact of the crash had created a gaping hole, like a tunnel. Inside was the cockpit and parts of the fuselage. Joining the team of rescuers were the two firemen who had put out the fire in the adjoining building. The first casualty was found by Paul, who climbed over the top of the deck to the plane. Unable to pry the top open, he called to Bill to bring him a crowbar. Ripping the top off, the men were curious by what they saw. It was a female passenger; what was curious was that among all the ruins surrounding her she's untouched by the debris. She was sitting in an upright position and her clothes were clean. Her body showed no evidence of abrasion, her expression peaceful. A fireman suddenly emerged from the tunnel and waved the first team to go in.

An eerie feeling gripped my soul as the first team came out of the tunnel with a body, covered with a green blanket. Their faces showed some fear, presumably of what they had seen remaining in the tunnel. And while order prevailed within the crowd, there were many still in shock and shaken by the events. The view paralyzed most of us, as bodies continued to be extricated from the tunnel of the church. Every time a body was carried out I followed it with my eyes as the men carried it to the gas station half a block away. It was like a caravan, circling in and out of the church and into the makeshift morgue at the gas station, its sign bearing the name Texaco visible among the smoke in the air. A woman, still in her night clothes, was screaming in a foreign language at a policeman, pointing to a store. The confused officer tried to calm her, to no avail, as she frantically tugged at him to come with her. He called out to a fireman, but the man was busy giving instruction to his men inside the church. The cop took the lady by her hand and literally dragged her to him. I could hear their conversation, as they were so close to me, in her broken English, she told them while pointing to the middle of the street that her husband who owned a butcher shop was missing. The fireman took his walkie-talkie and made a call; within minutes, two firefighters, the same ones who were on the roof of the adjoining building, came out of the church. I could hear their conversations, as they were ordered to go with the woman. I decided to abandon my place and follow them.

Across the East River, another rescue was taking form, as friends and neighbors of my parents had gathered at the store and at our residence as news of my whereabouts had spread like a wildfire. In the grocery store, plans were already underway to head into Brooklyn to search for me. My father was padlocking the front of the gate, as Mr. Alma brought his car, a pale blue 52 Chevy, around to pick up my father. Their plan was to pick up my mother and another friend who wanted to help. Mr. Alma had moved to the Lower East Side at about the same time we had. He had seen me grow along with his two sons, who went to school with me. He was always polite to my family, and my father considered him his best friend. Blowing the horn, Mr. Alma waived to my father and to Mr. Ortiz, another loyal friend and my father's dominoes partner. The roads were wet and slippery and traffic crawled, making the trip across the Manhattan Bridge seems interminable. Inside the Chevy, all you could hear were the wipers against the windshield, a haunting sound. In the backseat, my parents stared out across the river into Brooklyn. From the bridge up ahead, they could hear the sound of sirens and a gripping sensation came over the four of them and they wondered what lay ahead. Mr. Alma pointed out a huge cloud of smoke settling above a wide span of the city, and turning around, gave a look of concern to my parents.

At the approach ramp to the bridge, a policeman was directing all traffic into Brooklyn to the right, giving rescue vehicles priority to the crash site. Mr. Alma rolled down the window, and in broken English explained to the officer their situation. Looking in the back of the car toward my parents, the policeman explained that he had from his sergeant to redirect all traffic to the right. He added, though, that Mr. Alma could park his car next to the cruiser, and they could walk the twenty blocks to the crash site. He explained that all traffic was banned from the crash area. After consulting with each other, the four decided to take the officer's advice as they parked the car and began their long and cold journey toward the crash site.

As for me, I was much too wrapped up into this horrible event, and the thought that the news of this incident would have reached my parents didn't even enter my mind, nor did the store and the work I was supposed to do there. It was now four o'clock in the afternoon. I remember looking up and witnessing a glimpse of the sun as it slowly sank on the horizon, leaving behind a dark-blue sky, a reminder that night was about to commence. It had been over six hours, and with the exception of bodies being removed, the debris which shattered this neighborhood was still very visible; the main attraction was the huge tail, staring back at all those who stared at it.

Kings County Morgue
Brooklyn
4:01 p.m.

Kings County Hospital sent four ambulances, twenty-four doctors, eight nurses, and eight attendants to the crash site in Brooklyn's Park Slope section. A score of city and volunteer hospitals in Brooklyn also sent ambulances and doctors to Sterling Place, but there was little for them to do. The scene had now shifted to the hospital's morgue, as members of the victims waited in a private room, waiting for their names to be called, and when they were, they would go through the painful process of trying to identify their loved ones. Mayor Robert Wagner arrived to console the families, who were still in the early stages of mourning. Among the grieving was Mordine Mallory; she had just arrived and was desperate to get to a phone to inquire about her mother, who had been stricken by her son's tragedy. She approached a nurse's aide who escorted her to a private room for the call. Also in the crowd was a grief-stricken father by the name of George LaRiviere. Mr. LaRiviere, who is Eastern Regional Manager for the Electro-Motive Division of General Motors Corporation, had arranged to have his daughter Peggy and her friend Anne Hodgins come east for the holidays. The girls were freshmen at Barat College in Illinois. The three were supposed to leave Chicago aboard American Airlines back to New York's Idlewild Airport, but because they were unable to get seats aboard the American Airline flight they took the next plane available United 826. Mr. LaRiviere went ahead on the American flight, and promise to meet them there. He learned of the crash while waiting for them at the airport.

Mordine Mallory, in the little private room, called home.

"Hello Dad, this is Mordine, how is mom?"

"She's not doing too well, Mordine. Where are you?"

"I'm here in Brooklyn's Kings County Hospital. That's where they're bringing the victims."

"Any news?"

"No, Dad, not yet. They haven't called my name."

Just then she felt a light touch on her shoulder. It was the security guard, advising her that she was next. The words you're next repeated over and over in her mind, as the anxiety and grief knotted in her stomach.

Leaving the private room, she was faced with a long and narrow hallway of the hospital, at the very end of which she could see the doors to the morgue.

Her heart pounded inside her chest; her knees were weak. Trying to maintain her composure, Mordine held on to her black pocketbook, the only thing she carried. She squeezed it until she couldn't squeeze it anymore. To her, the walk seemed like that of a prisoner taking his last walk. Two things in her mind stood out, her brother Darnell, and her mom, Annie-Lou. Her biggest concern was how to tell her family that her brother was among the dead. Getting closer to the silver doors, Mordine began to feel a bit nauseous. The guard walking next to her showed no expression, but deep inside, he too felt pain for all of the victims and their family members. At the doors, Mordine stopped briefly; her fears were getting the best of her. Bending over to clear her head, she fought to maintain her balance, but her knees gave out. The guard grabbed her by her left arm, but it was too late and she crumbled to the hospital floor.

Hospital attendants, seeing what had just happened, raced over; the guard knelt by her side. Within seconds, she was surrounded by medics and others, like her, waiting to identify loved ones. One of the doctors suggested that she wait awhile before entering the morgue, but she politely refused. She wanted to get it over with so she could head to New Jersey to be with her grieving family.

With the help of the medic Mordine and the nervous guard, she walked to the silver doors. She stood before them for a moment, preparing herself for the worst. She had never gone through this, and she was worried about how she was going to react once she viewed the remains of her beloved brother. "Was his body mangled? Was there anything missing? Was his face recognizable?"

Looking at the concerned guard, she motioned him to go. The guard opened the immense doors and she stepped in. She was horrified by what she saw, full of bodies, all in black body bags. Each was on a chrome-like table. A nurse waited to help Mordine with the agonizing task of searching, bag by bag, for her little brother.

Across the way, in Methodist Hospital, Mr. and Mrs. Baltz, the parents of eleven-year-old Steven, arrived. Mr. Baltz, on hearing of the crash in his hometown of Wilmette, had taken the first plane out to be with his son. He was met at the hospital by his wife, Phyllis, and their daughter, Randee, who were privately escorted to the hospital from the airport by United Airline officials.

The three were now being escorted by the New York Police into the hospital wing, where their son lay in critical condition. The media had camped outside the compound of the hospital to get statements from the family of the only survivor of the plane crash. There was urgency and confusion, as nurses and doctors ran in and out of the boy's room. Even other patients were willing to wait so the staff could concentrate on saving the boy who, as they put it, came down from heaven. Arriving on the floor, Mr. Baltz was greeted by a staff of doctors in charge of the youngster's care. They were also met by the hospital chaplain, who helped comfort them and Randee, who seemed particularly worried and confused. She was immediately escorted by a nurse to a private room, while her parents spoke to officials from the police department and the Civil Aeronautics Board. Although security was supposed to be tight, a group of photographers made their way into the hospital, and when they saw the grieving parent's flashbulbs rang out, catching them by surprise and adding to the dismay of everyone.

Within seconds the police took control of the situation allowing Mr. and Mrs. Baltz to continue their interview with the officials.

Outside Steven's room were also the three men who had rescued him, there to see how the little guy, as they called him, was doing. Louis Viericki had been the first to reach Steven after the crash. He told reporters outside the hospital that seconds after the impact he saw a kid with his clothes on fire struggling toward the snow embankment by the plane's tail. Louis rushed to aid the boy, whose hair and face had been burned. His left hand seemed to be fractured because of the way he kept holding it up, Louis later reported, but he was still conscious. He picked Steven up and placed him on the snowbank and rolled him around. The other two were off duty police officers John Pihlaar and John O'Donnell. They were on their way to start their shift when they saw Louis attending to the bleeding kid and jumped out to help. After getting blankets from tenants, one of the officers picked up the boy and the three men raced six blocks to Methodist Hospital. They were still there, holding vigil, when Mr. Baltz approached them with his hand extended. He had heard of their heroic act and wanted to thank them personally on behalf of his family.

Louis looked at Mrs. Phyllis and said, "The little guy just kept asking for you. He kept saying I want my mommy. Where is my mommy?"

With those words, Mrs. Baltz collapsed against her husband and began to weep. Steven Baltz, age eleven, would die the next day from severe burns to his body, and complications of the lungs.

Sterling Place
Brooklyn, NY
December 16

The temperature had started to drop, and the cold made its way past my wet clothes and into my skin. It had been over six hours since I'd seen shelter and I was tired and hungry, but my fear had begun to subside. By now, crowd control had been secured and a barricade was installed around the crash site so there were no more people just roaming around; the crowd was contained outside of the site. Only official personnel were allowed to enter the wreckage, which still lay in pieces, just as it had landed that morning. The sun had set, leaving the city dark and the sky a dark navy blue. Two cranes were at work removing part of the building next to the church, which was in danger of collapsing, and two huge lamps had been set up over the Pillar of Fire Church as recovery was still in progress.

For the first time, I thought of my situation. I knew that I'd be in trouble back home and I had a lot of explaining to do. No sooner had I thought of that than a painful crack on the back of my head bought me to attention. It was my mother, who then grabbed me by my left ear and almost seemed to try to tear it off. She was hysterical, yelling at me but at the same time squeezing me close to her, as if to say, "Thank you, Lord." Despite the trouble I was in, I was happy and relieved to see her. Hugging her back, I saw my father out of the corner of my eye. He was walking toward me with Mr Alma and Mr. Ortiz. They reminded me of three sheriffs on their way to make an arrest. Dad didn't say much, nor did his two accomplices. He looked at my mother and in Spanish said to her, "Is he all right?" She nodded, "Yes."

It was over. It was finally over, and I was heading home. As I walked away from the crash site, I stopped to look one more time at all the destruction left behind by one single plane, one single event, the lives that it took, and the lives it changed. Sitting in the backseat of the car in the middle of the Brooklyn Bridge on my way home, I couldn't stop thinking of what happened there. You could still hear the sirens as ambulances continued their way to and from the site.

I went to bed without eating. I couldn't eat. I was still trembling from the cold, from what I had gone through, and from what was coming. From my bedroom window, I could see Brooklyn, and I wondered what was going on there. I also looked at what had been Joaquin's window before he was taken away, and I wondered how he was. I never found the bike store, although years later I found out that the store was in the Bronx, not Brooklyn.

For days, my father didn't talk to me. He was upset at my behavior and how I had let him down. But mostly he was upset by what I had put my mother through. On Christmas Eve, though, we finally talked. I was reading a comic book in bed, and he came in and stood there for a moment. He picked up the raccoon tails that were on the night table and said angrily in Spanish, "You disappointed me, Raymond. You lied to me and your mother. Although we are a poor family, we have always provided for you and gave you everything that your heart desired. We made sacrifices for you. Do you have anything to say to your mother or me?"

I bowed my head. "I'm sorry, Dad," was all I could say.

He looked at me for a moment; then continued.

"Right now what I want you to do is go into your mother's bedroom and apologize to her, but before you do, I want you to know that your punishment will be no bike this year, so I'm taking these raccoon tails because you won't need them. You're very lucky. It's only that. Now go and apologize to your mother."

I went to bed feeling guilty and bad that I had lied. I wasn't mad about my punishment. In fact, I felt pretty lucky; it could have been much worse. I was having trouble falling asleep, and kept tossing and turning. I got up to go to the bathroom and heard my parents talking. I thought it was very late and wondered why they were up. I opened the door a crack and there, to my amazement, was my bike: a Schwinn, with a cherry red frame, chrome fenders, and the raccoon tails hanging on each side of the bar. I thought I'd be so happy, but I didn't even smile. I only rode the bike once and then parked it in my bedroom, where it stayed until my father sold it. The bike just didn't matter anymore.

Hartford, CT
December 13, 2001

In three days, it will be forty-one years since that horrific day on a quiet street in Brooklyn. Perhaps because of recent events, or perhaps because the weather today is what it was forty-one years ago, I am haunted again by those memories. I think of all the people who died on those planes and I can't help but wonder what they thought just before impact, and how they felt when they knew their destiny was sealed. I think of Darnell, Vincent, and Arthur, and I think of that little boy. I think of their families, and the pain they had endured. And I wonder about it all now more than ever. At the time, how or why it happened didn't really matter to me. To me, it was just a day of horror, chaos, and death, something I never could have fathomed. The destruction that one jet caused was unbelievable, and the lives that were lost could never be comprehended.

I have often wondered why I was put in such a situation. "Who makes those decisions? Is it the Creator or is it his Opponent? And for what purpose? Why are we placed in a transgression scene, when all we were doing was going to the grocery store? Why are we put in a sinking ship, when all we wanted was a peaceful and quiet vacation? Why are we placed in a doomed plane, when all we wanted was to get home to our loved ones? Is disaster part of life? Is it something that we all should fear and respect? And who decides whether you will be victim or witness?"

The victims are gone, some forgotten. Their lives and dreams were obliterated in a flash, leaving their souls to linger. Death does not discriminate; it isn't interested in age, color, or gender. It demeans the message, the faith, and the hope given to us by our parents and passed to them by their own parents. We cannot understand death's choices.

"And what of the witnesses, left behind to remember? Why were they spared? What is their mission? Is there a mission?"

The following excerpts are from the actual transcript of the final moments of both planes, taken from the Civil Aeronautics Board. Some of the findings I found very disturbing.

CIVIL AERONAUTICS BOARD
File No. 1-0083
Adopted: June 12, 1962
Released: June 18, 1962
United Air Lines, Inc., DC-8 N 8013U
Trans World Airlines, Inc., Constellation 1049A, N 6907C
Near Staten Island, New York, December 16, 1960

Synopsis

On December 16, 1960, at 1033, EST, a collision between Trans-World Airlines Model 1049A Constellation, N6907C, and a United Air Lines DC-8 N 8013U, occurred near Miller Army Air Field, Staten Island, New York. Trans World Airlines flight 266 originated at Dayton, Ohio. The destination was LaGuardia Airport, New York, with one en route stop at Columbus, Ohio. United Air Lines flight 826 was a nonstop service originating at O'Hare Airport, Chicago, Illinois, with its destination New York International Airport, New York. Both aircraft were operating under Instrument Flight Rules. Following the collision, the Constellation fell on Miller Army Filed, and the DC-8 continued in a northeasterly direction, crashing into Sterling Place near Seventh Avenue in Brooklyn, New York. Both aircraft were totally destroyed. All 128 occupants of both aircraft and five persons on the ground in Brooklyn were fatally. There was considerable damage to property in the area of the ground of the DC-8.

TWA flight 266 departed Port Columbus Airport at 0900, operating routinely under Air Traffic Control into the New York area. The New York Route traffic Control Center.

(ARTCC) subsequently advised that radar contact had been established, and cleared the flight to the Linden intersection. Control of the flight was subsequently transferred to LaGuardia Approach Control. When the flight was about over the Linden Intersection, LaGuardia Approach Control began vectoring TWA 266 by radar to the final approach course for a landing on runway four at LaGuardia. Shortly thereafter TWA 266 was cleared to descend to five thousand feet, and was twice advised of traffic in the vicinity on a northeasterly heading. Following the transmission of this information the radar targets appeared to merge on the LaGuardia Approach Control radar scope and communication with TWA 266 were lost.

United Air Lines flight 826 operated routinely between Chicago and the New York area, contacting the New York ARTCC at 10:12 a.m. Shortly thereafter the New York Center cleared United 826 to proceed from Allentown, Pa., very high frequency omni directional radio range station (VOR) direct to the Robbinsville, New Jersey, VOR, and then to the Preston Intersection via Victor Airway 123.

At approximately 10:21 a.m., UAL 826 contacted Aeronautical Radio, Inc. (ARINC to advise their company that the No. 2 receiver accessory unit was inoperative, which would indicate that one of the aircraft's two VHF radio navigational receivers was not functioning. A fix is established by the intersection of two radials from two separate radio range stations. With one unit inoperative, the cross-bearing necessary can be taken by tuning the remaining receiver from one station to the other. This process consumes considerable time, however, and is not as accurate as the simultaneous display of information on two separate position deviation indicators. While UAL 826 advised the company that one unit was inoperative, Air Traffic Control was not advised. At 10:25 a.m., the New York ARTCC issued a clearance for a new routing which shortened the distance to Preston by approximately eleven miles. As a result, this reduced the amount of time available to the crew to retune the single radio receiver to either the Colt's Neck, New Jersey, or Solberg, New Jersey, VOR in order to establish the cross bearing with Victor 123, which would identify the Preston Intersection. In the event, the crew would not attempt to retune the single VOR receiver, cross bearing on the Scotland Low Frequency Radio-beacon could be taken with the aircraft direction finding (ADF) equipment.

This would be a means of identifying the Preston Intersection but, under the circumstances, would require rapid mental calculation in the interpretation of a display which could be easily misread. Several factors support the conclusion that this occurred. Instructions had been issued to United 826 for holding at the Preston Intersection, the clearance limit, should holding be necessary. Clearance beyond Preston for an approach to Idlewild Airport would be received from Idlewild Approach Control and the transfer of control of the flight from the New York Center to Idlewild Approach control would normally take place as the aircraft was approaching Preston. UAL 826 was not receiving radar vectors, but was providing its own navigation. After the flight reported passing through six thousand feet, the New York Center advised that radar service was terminated, and instructed the flight to contact Idlewild Approach Control. UAL 826 then called Idlewild Approach Control, stating

"United 826 approaching Preston at five thousand."

This was the last known transmission from UAL 826.

At the time United 826 advised it was approaching Preston, it had in fact gone on by this clearance limit several seconds before, and was several miles past the point at which it should have turned into the holding pattern. This is confirmed by the data obtained from the flight recorder which had been installed in the UAL DC-8, as well as by analysis of the communication tapes. At a point approximately eleven miles past the Preston intersection, the collision occurred. Based on the flight recorder aboard 826 and wheels-off time for 826 at Chicago of 9:11 a.m., the collision occurred at approximately 10:33:33 a.m. There is also evidence based upon sounds heard by the radio at the LaGuardia tower that the collision occurred at that time. The physical fact makes it apparent that United 826 had already proceeded past the Preston Intersection at the time the radar controller terminated radar service just seconds before the collision, but the controller did nothing. When 826 proceeded past its Preston clearance limit, it was an obvious deviation. Yet the radar controller who had not yet terminated radar service made no effort to call and advise 826 of this crucial fact. That morning flight 826 was the only aircraft in the vicinity at the time. If the controller was performing his duties and maintaining radar separation and radar service, why was not a warning issued to United 826? Both Idlewild radar controllers stated that they did not see 826 in the Preston area on their radar scope. They took no steps at the time to search for 826. At the time of 826's call, Idlewild Approach Control did not receive any communication from New York Center, that control of the trip was being transferred. The primary method of communication for transfer of control interphone was not used. Apparently, the secondary means of transfer, switching lights, was not properly utilized because Approach Control did not receive any light signal from the Center.

In fact, Approach Control had to request a switch of the lights after 826 made the initial radio contact with the Approach facility. When Approach Control received the call from 826 at 10:33:28 a.m., five minutes prior to the posted ETA, the radar controller did not locate the aircraft on their radar scope and took no steps to attempt to locate it until after LaGuardia Approach Control indicated the possibility of a midair collision.

This factual presentation makes it abundantly clear that 826 was still under radar control and receiving radar service by the New York Air Route Traffic Control Center from 10:22:41 until 10:33:27. During this period, radar separation should have been utilized, but for reasons unknown, it wasn't.

The other troubling fact was the re-routing of United 826 to short cut the Victor 30 airway to Victor 123 and to Preston was apparently the first that the radar controller had given on that morning of the accident. As stated previously in my investigation, this deviation from standard established routing was not a published procedure and was not contained in the letter of agreement between Air Traffic Control facilities, nor was it specified anywhere in the arrival routes set forth in the notice given by the New York Center to all pilots. The re-routing of 826 not only altered the time, distance, and course to the Preston Intersection, but, more importantly, superimposed upon the crew an additional burden than what they already had set in front of them. Just two months before, on October 26, 1960, the New York Center had assured all pilots that such last-minute changes would not occur, yet it did. In addition, traffic in the sector for that morning was not heavy, and even today no very good reason has been given as to why a shortcut was given. Why wasn't United 826 allowed to continue on its normal flight path? We may never know the truth. However, it's important to mention that since the date of the accident, the shortcut described above was never used again. It is also important to mention that on December 19, 1960, just three days after the accident, a joint meeting of all operating committees for both aircraft was held at the Federal Building at the Idlewild Airport to interview all FAA controllers who were involved. Controller Fred Prawdzik of the LaGuardia Approach Control stated that when he saw the unidentified target (826), he shouted a couple of times at the TWA radar controller about the presence of unidentified traffic but his calls went unanswered by the controller in charge.

Many of the documents produced by Air Traffic Control in this investigation contain language that attempts to minimize its obligations, duties, and responsibilities.

History of TWA 266

Trans-World Airlines Flight 266 was a scheduled passenger service originating at Dayton, Ohio. The destination was LaGuardia Airport, New York, with one en route stop at Columbus, Ohio. The crew consisted of Captain David A. Wollan, First Officer Dean T. Bowen, Flight Engineer LeRoy L. Rosenthal, and Hostesses Margaret Gernat and Patricia Post. During the stopover at Columbus, a scheduled equipment change was made. Flight 266 departed Port Columbus with the previous listed crew and thirty-nine passengers, including two infants. Flight 266 departed Port Columbus Airport at 0900 Eastern Standard Time. The gross weight at takeoff was 101,444 pounds including 2,600 gallons of fuel. The aircraft was within weight and balance limitations in accord with current procedures. The time en route to LaGuardia was estimated to be one hour and thirty-two minutes. The flight plan specified Instrument Flight Rules (IFR) at seven-thousand-foot altitude. The clearance was to the LaGuardia Airport via direct Appleton, Ohio; Victor 12 Johnstown, Pennsylvania; Victor 106 Selinsgrove, Pennsylvania; Victor 6, Victor 123 to LaGuardia Airport. Subsequent clearances changed the altitude to seventeen thousand feet, then to nineteen thousand feet. The flight was routine as it progressed toward the New York area. At approximately 10:05 a.m., flight 266 reported to the New York Air Route Control Center over Selinsgrove at nineteen thousand feet. Shortly thereafter, the New York Center cleared flight 266 to descend in stages, and to cross Allentown, Pennsylvania at eleven thousand feet. At 10:19 a.m., TWA 266 reported to the New York Center on 125.3 mcs that it was passing Allentown, at eleven thousand feet. In response, the New York Center advised that radar contact had been established, cleared the flight to Linden Intersection, and requested it to stand by for descent. At 10:21 a.m., New York Center further cleared TWA 266 to descend to and maintain ten thousand feet. The flight acknowledged this clearance and reported leaving eleven thousand feet. At 10:23 a.m., the New York Center advised the flight of the current LaGuardia weather: measured five hundred overcast: one mile visibility in light snow; surface wind northwest fifteen knots; altimeter setting 29.66. The flight acknowledged this weather and requested the runway in use. The Center advised that Instrument system (ILS) approaches were being made to runway four and that the localizer was inoperative.

Flight 266 acknowledged. Between 10:24 and 10:26 a.m., the New York Center cleared TWA 266 to descend to and maintain nine thousand and to report leaving ten thousand feet.

This was acknowledged. At 10:27 a.m., TWA 266 advised the Center that it was past Solberg, New Jersey VOR. The Center acknowledges. Shortly thereafter, New York Center advised that radar service was terminated and to contact LaGuardia Approach on 125.7 mcs. TWA acknowledges by repeating the frequency. TWA 266 reported to LaGuardia Approach Control on 125.7 mcs that it has passed Solberg at an altitude of nine thousand feet. The time correlated with the Center tape was 10:27:22 a.m.

LaGuardia Approach Control acknowledged, and issued the following clearance:

Maintain nine thousand feet; report the zero one zero Robbinsville, ILS runway four, landing four, no delay expected. The wind is northwest at 15; Altimeter 29.65. LaGuardia weather; measured five hundred overcast; visibility one mile; light snow, stand by.

TWA acknowledged the clearance. At 10:28 a.m., TWA 266 reported passing the zero one zero degree radial of Robbinsville and requested information on the LaGuardia localizer. LaGuardia Approach Control advised that the glide slope rather than the LaGuardia localizer was inoperative as had been previously reported and cleared the flight to eight hundred feet. TWA 266 acknowledged and reported leaving nine thousand. At 10:29 a.m., LaGuardia Approach Control cleared TWA 266 to descend to six thousand feet and to advise passing through eight thousand feet. The transmission was acknowledged. At 10:29:49 a.m., TWA 266 reported passing eight thousand. LaGuardia acknowledged and advised the flight to maintain present heading for radar vector to the final-approach course. TWA 266 acknowledged. At 10:30:49 a.m., LaGuardia Approach Control advised TWA 266 to reduce to approach speed. The flight acknowledged. At 10:32:09 a.m., LaGuardia Control advised TWA 266 to turn right to a heading of 130 degrees. The transmission was acknowledged by repeating the heading. LaGuardia Approach Control again advised that this would be a radar vector to the final approach course. TWA 266 acknowledged. LaGuardia Control then requested the flights altitude. At 10:32:20 a.m., the flight advised: six thousand. At 10:32:22 a.m., LaGuardia Approach acknowledged and cleared the flight to continue descent to five thousand. This clearance was acknowledged by the flight which then reported leaving six thousand feet. Approach Control acknowledged.

At 10:32:37 a.m., LaGuardia Approach Control advised the flight to turn right to 150 degrees. This was acknowledged from TWA 266 by repeating the heading.

At 10:32:47 a.m., LaGuardia Approach Control advised, Traffic at two thirty, six miles northeast-bound.

At 10:32:51 a.m., TWA 266 acknowledged. At 10:33:08 a.m., LaGuardia Approach Control requested the flight's altitude. TWA replied, (garbled) five hundred.

LaGuardia Approach Control asked if 5,500 was correct. TWA 266 replied affirmative. At 10:33:14 a.m., LaGuardia Approach issued clearance to continue descent to fifteen hundred. At 10:33:18 a.m., this was acknowledged. At 10:33:21 a.m., LaGuardia advised to A Turn left now heading 130.

At 10:33:23 a.m., TWA 266 acknowledged by repeating the heading.

At 10:33:26 a.m., LaGuardia Control advised, Roger, that appears to be a jet traffic off your right now at three o'clock at one mile, northeast-bound.

Following this transmission, at 10:33:33 a.m., a noise similar to that caused by an open microphone was heard for a six-second duration as LaGuardia Control tried frantically to contact TWA 266.

History of United 826

United Air Lines 826 was a scheduled nonstop passenger service originating at O'Hare Airport, in Chicago Illinois, with its destination New York International Airport, New York, New York. The crew consisted of Captain Robert E. Sawyer, First Officer Robert W. Fiebling, Second Officer Richard E. Prewitt, Stewardesses Mary J. Mahoney, Augustine L. Ferrar, Anne M. Bouthen, and Patricia A. Keller. The crew normally departed Los Angeles, California, as United Flight 856, with a two-hour stopover in Chicago, and departing Chicago as United Flight 826. Captain Sawyer, First Officer Fiebling, and Second Officer Prewitt had flown Flight 856 from Los Angeles to Chicago. They departed Los Angeles at approximately 3:20 a.m. on December 16, 1960, and arrived in Chicago at approximately 6:56 a.m. The stewardesses boarded united 826 at Chicago.

United 826 departed O'Hare Airport with the previously listed crew and seventy-seven passengers at 9:11 a.m. Cruising flight level at twenty-seven thousand feet was attained at 9:36 a.m. The flight to the New York area was normal. At approximately 10:12 a.m., New York Air Route traffic control was contacted by flight 826. The center answered.

"United 826, New York Center, roger, have you on progress, radar service available, descend to and maintain flight level 250, over." Flight 826 reported leaving 270 at approximately 10:14 a.m. At 10:15 a.m., New York Center advised, "United 826, clearance limit is Preston Intersection via jet 60 Victor to Allentown direct to Robbinsville, via Victor 123: maintain flight level 250."

Flight 826 acknowledged. At approximately 10:21 a.m., United 826 called ARINC (Aeronautical Radio, Inc.), the operator of United Air Lines Communication system, and reported No. 2 navigation receiver accessory unit, inoperative.

This transmission was acknowledged by ARINC and relayed to United Air Lines.

At approximately 10:21 a.m., New York Center issued further clearance to descend to thirteen thousand feet. United replied, "We'd rather hold upstairs."

Subsequent to this transmission, the United flight was instructed to change to 123.6 mcs, the frequency of another center sector controller. At approximately 10:22:41 a.m., the center called flight 826.

"United 826, New York Center radar contact."

"United replied, Roger, we're cleared to thirteen thousand to maintain twenty-five thousand until we had conversation with you. If we're going to have a delay, we would rather hold upstairs than down. We're going to need three-fourths of a mile. Do you have weather handy?"

The center replied, "No, but I'll get it. There has been no delay until now."

At approximately 10:23:30 a.m., United 826 reported over Allentown at flight level 250.

The center acknowledged. At 10:24:37 a.m., the center advised that Idlewild weather was fifteen hundred feet overcast; two mile; light rain; fog; altimeter setting 29.65.

Shortly thereafter, the flight stated, "We're starting down."

At approximately 10:25:09 a.m., the center amended the ATC clearance as follows: 826 cleared to proceed on Victor 30 until intercepting Victor 123 and that way to Preston. It'll be a little bit quicker. (The new route would shorten the distance to Preston by eleven miles.) This was acknowledged by United 826 at 10:25:20 a.m.

At approximately 10:26:49 a.m., the flight was cleared to descend to and maintain eleven thousand feet. The clearance was acknowledged and the flight reported leaving twenty-one thousand feet.

At approximately 10:28:41 a.m., the center advised, "United 826, A826, I show you crossing the centerline Victor at this time."

United 826 confirmed that it was established on Victor 30 and requested his distance from Victor 123. At approximately 10:28:56 a.m., the center said, "I show you fifteen, no, make it sixteen miles Victor 123."

United 826 acknowledged and then the center advised, "Right now, you're about two miles from crossing Victor Airways 433."

At approximately 10:30:07 a.m., United 826 was cleared to descend to and maintain five thousand feet. This was acknowledged and 826 reported leaving fourteen thousand feet. The center then asked, "Looks like you'll be able to make Preston at five thousand?"

The answer was that they would try. At approximately 10:32:16 a.m., the center stated, "United 826, if holding is necessary at Preston, southwest one-minute pattern right turns the only delay will be in your descent."

The flight replied, "Roger, no delay, we're out of seven."

At approximately 10:33:01 a.m., the flight reported passing six thousand feet.

At approximately 10:33:08 a.m., the center called, "826, I'm sorry I broke you up; was that your reporting leaving six thousand for five thousand?"

The flight replied, "Affirmative."

At approximately 10:33:20 a.m., New York Center instructed, "United, 826, roger, and you received the holding instructions at Preston, radar service is terminated, contact Idlewild Approach Control. Good day."

"Flight 826 acknowledged, Good day."

At approximately 10:33:28 a.m., (time taken from Idlewild Approach Control tape) United Flight 826 called, "Idlewild Approach Control United 826 approaching Preston at five thousand."

This was the last known transmission from flight 826.

At 10:33:35 a.m., Idlewild Approach Control issued the following transmission to United: "United 826, this is Idlewild Approach Control, maintain five thousand, little or no delay at Preston. Idlewild landing runway four right, ILS in use Idlewild weather, six hundred scattered. Estimate fifteen hundred overcast visibility two mile, light rain, and fog altimeter 29.63. Over."

The transmission was completed at approximately 10:33:54 a.m. It was not acknowledged. Several attempts to contact flight 826 were unsuccessful.

Findings of the Civil Aeronautics Board

On May 9, 1962, the Civil Aeronautics Board made its findings public. The Board determined that the probable cause of the collision was the United's crew misinterpretation of the available navigational instruments, thereby allowing the flight to exceed the confines of the allocated airspace. A contributing factor was the high rate of speed of the DC-8 as it approached the Preston Intersection, coupled with the change of clearance which reduced the en-route distance along Victor 123 by approximately eleven miles, causing the collision to occur.

Conclusion

I never went back to Sterling Place. It took me forty years to openly talk about it. I still get a chill every time I think of it or talk about it. I still think about all those bodies and the shattered dreams from above. Increasingly, though, I wondered why it happened not philosophically or spiritually, but mechanically.

Doing my research and getting information under the Freedom of Information Act, I obtained critical information about the crash. One source was the Civil Aeronautics Board. As I analyzed their report, it was clear that the crew of the United jet was at fault. But it was also clear, to me, that the accident could have been prevented. For reasons unknown, not everyone was doing their job that day. United Flight 826 had violated the clearance limit at Preston and as a result, proceeded beyond it by approximately eleven miles, where it collided with TWA Flight 266, at approximately five thousand feet, sending the Constellation plane, which was flying in accordance with its clearance and instructions given by LaGuardia Approach Control, and its forty-four occupants into a spiraling death. The exact reason for United proceeding beyond Preston is not known with any degree of certainty, but in all probability it was because of (1) a navigational error by the crew, or (2) a failure of navigational equipment, either in the air or on the ground. Although it is technically true that the accident would not have occurred if United had not violated its limit of clearance, it is also true that FAA Radar Controllers could have prevented the accident had one of three things been avoided.

(1) The New York Air Traffic Controllers failed to notice that United Flight 826 had passed more than eleven miles beyond the limit of the Preston holding pattern fix at 10:33:20 a.m., leaving the crew to do

their own navigation, under IFR conditions zero visibility. The FAA Manual, however, provides the following: Approach deviations from standard or normal flight paths, or other flight information observed on the radar-scope, *should be transmitted to the pilot immediately*, to be used at his discretion. Despite the fact that radar service had not been terminated and Flight 826 had passed the Preston Intersection, the radar controller did not advise 826 of their deviation.

(2) Idlewild Approach Control failed to observe the position of United Flight 826 on its radar-scope at 10:33:28 a.m. when 826 made its only radio contact with Idlewild, seconds before the collision. According to the transcripts from the Civil Aeronautics Board, it was not until the approximately 10:33:33 a.m. time of impact that Idlewild responded. If this is true, my question is: "Where was the controller? Was he at his station, or was he just getting there?"

Remember, Idlewild Approach Control never acknowledged target (U826) on radar, to either New York Center or to the crew of Flight 826) (A target is a blip on a radar-scope. Each blip represents a moving object, and each object is a target with a flight number, in this case U826.)

(3) The most damaging and disturbing evidence of neglect lies with the controllers at LaGuardia that day. On *two occasions,* LaGuardia Approach Control observed an unidentified target (Flight 826) on its radar-scope but failed to provide evasive maneuvers to TWA Flight 266. The fact that an unidentified target appeared in the high-density LaGuardia vectoring area should have immediately alerted the Air Traffic Controller to the possibility of a collision (a red flag). The LaGuardia controller should have identified or attempted to identify the target and to have immediately provided evasive vectors for TWA 266. Had the New York controller properly vectored, United 826 until Idlewild confirmed, taking over flight instead of terminating flight without confirmation, then it's very possible the collision would not have occurred. It is my strong opinion that had all three controllers done their jobs according to policy, manuals, *and* common sense, had they done their best for the crew and passengers who were flying in a difficult situation, this accident would have never occurred.

A Word About My Research

The story you just read is true. Contents of this story were taken from the files of the Civil Aeronautics Board, The National Archives of Maryland, and newspaper clippings from The Hartford Public Library in Connecticut. Some scenes were created, not to sensationalize the story but to convey the impact of the tragedy. Other scenes were witnessed by this author, on that day. Some of the families whose loved ones were mentioned in this book were unavailable for comment, despite repeated efforts to locate and contact them. One family declined to be interviewed, stating that they were still grieving. Some names were changed to honor the wishes of the relevant people.

It is very important to me, then, to express my gratitude to all those who allowed me to tell their stories. I want to thank the Mallory family for letting me into their blessed home for the interview, to Ms. Gloria Fowler for her candid telephone interview, and special thanks to Mr. Paul Geidel for his openness as we compared notes.

I also want to strongly express that while my conclusion as to the cause of this accident may differ from those of others, it is my view of this accident only, and should not be taken as detracting from the fine work of the men and women in our aviation agencies. As a pilot, I am well aware of the overall excellence in the industry.

My reason for including portions of the actual transcripts is to enable you to decide for yourself why this accident took place and whether it could have been prevented.

Last, I would like to say that I did not write this book to garner riches or fame, but to finally express what I had witnessed and what I've learned from the experience. It is my wish that proceeds from this book go to the families of the loved ones whose stories I have told herein.

For Paul

On the morning of September 11, 2001, the United States was attacked by a terrorist group. Four commercial jets were hijacked, two crashed into the World Trade Center. The entire force of the Fire Department of New York was called out. Rescue One, was one of the first to arrive, Paul Geidel's son, Gary, who in 1960 as a child wanted to be a fireman like his daddy, achieved his dream and became a fireman with Rescue One.

As terrified people ran out from the Trade Center, Gary raced in; an in doing so, was one of the 343 firemen who gave the ultimate sacrifice, his life.

Made in United States
North Haven, CT
22 February 2023

33035361R00118